Robak's Fire

Robak's Fire

JOE L. HENSLEY

PUBLISHED FOR THE CRIME CLUB BY
DOUBLEDAY & COMPANY, INC.
GARDEN CITY, NEW YORK
1986

Library of Congress Cataloging-in-Publication Data

Hensley, Joe L., 1926–
Robak's fire.

I. Title.
PS3558.E55R65   1986   813'.54   86-8853
ISBN 0-385-23359-0
Copyright © 1986 by Joe L. Hensley
All Rights Reserved
Printed in the United States of America
First Edition

Robak's Fire

CHAPTER ONE

Robak's Rule: "When there's a rotten smell in Denmark, it may spread into the nearby counties."

One side of the steep road that led from the south down to Drewville was tree-lined and there were still more than a few brown sere leaves hanging on branches, dappling the warm sunlight. It had been a very good autumn, slow and gentle and without, as yet, any bitter-cold weather. Most of the leaves had turned color in late September and fallen during mid-October rains. Now it was later in October and I could almost taste the odors of autumn; the dust of harvested corn, the annual death smell of green things mixed with the scent of burning leaves.

It was a county-election fall (aren't most of them?), and the October trees and telephone poles were burdened with the bright imploring signs of candidates. I saw a dozen "Keeler for Judge" signs, fewer for his opponent, someone named Howard Jay. Keeler was the judge trying the case I'd come about.

I'd driven the road one time before, and it had kept me alert then also. It was full of hairpin turns, and it descended at an alarming grade from a high hill down into the alluvial valley below. It was a twenty-mile-an-hour road. The aging LTD's tires squealed and the brakes protested, but the car and I arrived alive and together in the valley.

Drewville lay there beside the Blue River, a stream much prized in spring and summer by canoeists and rafters and all year long by fishermen. Farther downstream the Blue widened, slowed, and then emptied into the muddy Ohio, but here in the valley it was a narrow rapid river, running along the near side of the road, not very deep in the dry fall. At the city limits there was a newly painted bright-yellow bridge. I crossed the river there. The highway down into the valley had been almost deserted, and so was the main street of Drewville.

I knew a bit about the recent history of Drewville. Two years back they'd shut down work on a huge nuclear plant near where the Blue met the Ohio. There'd been sit-ins and protests earlier from those into that sort of thing, plus complaints to the Nuclear Regulatory Commission by the disgruntled and alarmed, but they hadn't stopped the plant. The planners themselves had decided the eventual cost of building the plant would be too expensive. Ten thousand people had lost high-paying jobs. Now all there was at the nuclear plant were the rusting shells of two containment towers and half-completed construction on auxiliary buildings, with a few bored guards patrolling the ruins. I'd seen the plant site from the road ten miles back before climbing into the hills.

Drewville, when the nuclear plant closed, had gone into collective shock and, like other towns near the construction site, never fully recovered. The closing had emptied houses and stopped construction on others. It had closed a vast trailer park and stopped work on a new shopping center, the latter looking fire-damaged, as if it had burned after construction ceased. I saw those skeletons as I drove up the street. The town now had many "For Sale" signs on empty houses and a plethora of boarded-up commercial buildings.

I drove straight along the main street until I found the Valley Motel. I checked in there. An alert, wise-eyed old lady at the desk was cheerful enough in furnishing my key. The motel was run down, but clean and cheap. Along the far side there was the beginning of another wing, the footings laid, the first course of cement blocks up, but now grown mossy and discolored. Probably a nuclear-plant casualty.

The air conditioner in my window made a moaning sound when I turned it on, but then settled into sluggish, silent activity. My partners, Jake and Sam, already in residence, had told Steinmetz, my semi-retired partner, that the Valley Motel was the best in town, that I should come there, check in, and then contact them secretly.

I'd been intrigued when Steinmetz had told me that. He'd been intrigued to tell me, grinning his crease-necked, bald-headed grin, shaking his wise old head. He was now "of counsel" to the firm, which meant he came into the office anytime he wanted and kept no hours and could be seen only by appointment. That was about the way it had been when he was a full partner. But he liked being listed as "of counsel" on the sign outside the office door, and if it pleased him, it pleased me. I was very fond of the old man.

"What have we got you into now, Robak?" he'd asked when he shook his head.

"Lord knows," I'd answered darkly. "I can't see Jake in trouble. He's so damned self-sufficient."

Steinmetz had smiled. "He needs you because you're mean and righteous. I'm a lawyer because it's a profession, a way of life. You're a lawyer because you want to right wrongs and find the truth. You're dangerous more because you're stubborn than because you're good." Then he'd laughed a little, taking some of the sting out of his words.

I thought he'd meant them.

And so I'd gone. I'd said good-bye to Jo, my wife, and my son Joe, now aged three. I'd told Jo it was a "civil matter" I was going to Drewville on, something other than a criminal thing, and that had relieved her mind some. She didn't care a lot for some of my criminal cases. When it got right down to it, neither did I. I'd started getting disenchanted with them around my fortieth birthday. My problem was I continued to take them because I was still curious.

Jo had wondered, if it was a civil case, what I was doing going off to it on a Friday, telling her I'd be gone the weekend. I'd said I didn't know for sure, but that they wanted me in Drewville that afternoon. I told her I'd call or return on Sunday. I'd found that she and Joe did quite well when I was gone, that they were sufficient company for each other.

I walked from the motel to the Drew County courthouse. It sat in the middle of a block of land in downtown Drewville. The town itself was a dusty and dingy wide spot in the road of (now) maybe three to four thousand people. I'd seen the hillside and bottom farmland around the town when I was driving in. Poor land, gray rather than brown or black, good enough for a nuclear plant, but bad for farming. I doubted you could raise hell on it with two blondes and a full barrel of whiskey. This year's best crop had probably been the bumper harvest of political signs I'd seen coming down the hill. *Vote, and please vote for me.*

They had the back doors to the courtroom open and there were no empty seats inside. Crowded courtrooms, these days, are the exception rather than the rule unless the trial concerns a bizarre murder or someone rich and/or infamous. The civil case Jake and Sam were defending had gotten a lot of media attention. Some people stood at the back doors and I joined them. They looked me over curiously, decided I was merely a *not much* curiosity-seeker, and then grudgingly made a place for me because I was large and apparently intended to have one. I was dressed like a nonlawyer in rumpled cords and a faded wool shirt.

Up front I could see Jake and Sam sitting at their counsel table. They seemed angry and I assumed they'd just lost an argument about admissibility. The six-person jury was examining what appeared to be photographs. I couldn't make out exactly what they were photos of from my vantage point, but from the jury's attitude while looking them over they weren't pleasant pictures from someone's family album.

At the opposing counsel table a thin, gray lawyer sat easily, his manner confident. I'd been told his name, but had forgotten it. *Linden? No, Lennon, Damon Lennon.*

The judge, whose full name was Amos Keeler, was watching a wall clock impatiently. He was a florid man, dressed in a black funeral-director-type suit. He was sixtyish and affected a gold chain across his vest. A bull of a man who liked the power of his job, I thought. That was his reputation, according to Steinmetz.

"You got to watch him pretty careful, Don," Steinmetz had warned. "He's tricky and he's got his fingers in lots of pies around that county. At judges' meetings I used to hear stories about him. He likes to put people in jail for contempt. Show his power. We called him 'Iron Hand' to his back and laughed at him, but I'd doubt a lawyer practicing before him should do that."

It was almost four on a Friday, the witching hour in most small county courtrooms. In my own county of Mojeff I'd have bet you could have fired a cannon down the middle of the upstairs hall and have injured no one at this hour.

I tired of not knowing exactly what was transpiring inside, and so I parted the crowd again and walked back to the motel and waited. I turned on the television and flipped the channel selector. All I could find were soap operas and a Western so old, John Wayne looked boyish. I had a bottle of emergency V.O. in the bag and there was ice at the end of the building, but I decided against a drink. Instead I turned off the TV and took a long, singing shower in lukewarm water, dressed, and found a Burger King full of grade and high school kids. I got a Whopper and black coffee and ate them there, ignoring the noise from the kids and their satchel radios.

By the time I returned, it was full dark. No one seemed to

be watching, but I went out and took a brisk walk around the motel and its unfinished addition in the darkness anyway. I looked things over carefully. I didn't see anyone, but I wasn't sure there wasn't someone out there. Coming back past Jake and Sam's room, I tapped lightly on the door. Sam opened it a crack and smiled at me.

"Anyone see you?" he asked conspiratorially.

"I don't know. Eventually they're going to put me together with you guys, but no one seems to be watching me now. I guess."

Sam shook his head.

"There will be," Jake advised carefully from behind Sam. "Well, come on inside, for crap's sake."

Their motel room was furnished in old hickory-modern, like mine. Jake sat on one bed drinking morosely from a dark-brown drink.

"Steinmetz said you guys called and wanted me to come here for a couple of days," I said. "Now one of you needs to tell me more about the why. All I know is that Steinmetz said some people named Benjamin had sued two insurance companies. I read some newspaper stuff about that. A lot of money involved. Some guy did or didn't burn up in a home fire?"

Jake nodded and pointed me at a chair. He and I had been law partners for a number of years without a major disagreement, but that was mostly because he went his way and I went mine. My business normally made him nervous. His usually bored me. He did civil cases, wills and estates. He represented insurance companies and corporations. He was good at it. And he was honest and did a first-class job running the office.

"Something's wrong here," Jake said. "Sam and I wanted you to look it over this weekend while we go back to Bington. Did you get your press card from the Bington paper?"

I nodded. On the promise I'd charge him nothing unless I

wrote something he deemed suitable, the editor of the Bington *Chronicle* had "hired" me as a reporter to cover the trial. My press card read "Brockton Publications," which was the corporate entity that owned the *Chronicle* and seven or eight other area papers. A nice, anonymous card. They'd even managed to misspell my last name on it so that I was one D. Robbak. I didn't know whether that was on purpose or by accident. Now and then, when they leaned on me in the newspaper, they spelled it right enough.

"The case keeps sliding out from under us," Sam said. "Two insurance companies refused to pay death benefits, and the widow and two sons by a previous marriage, being the heirs of the alleged deceased, one Avery Benjamin, filed this action two years back. It just kind of lay there for a long while and the local lawyer who represented the insurance companies didn't seem much worried about it."

"So what happened?"

"The plaintiffs started howling early this year and got it set for trial. That was when we got into it. There's in excess of a million and a half on the policies, but punitive damages could add up to five million more. We had some witnesses who gave us statements that they saw the deceased alive after he was supposed to have died in a fire at his home. Now, suddenly, we don't have them anymore, but we do have some insurance companies who aren't very happy with us or with the justice system. We've got a judge who's giving us fits. He lets the plaintiffs do about as they like and reads us off every chance he gets. More than that, he's told us he won't let us impeach our own witnesses in front of the jury. Everything we want to do so far he doesn't want us to do."

"Steinmetz talked some about him," I said. "He said when he was judging and would come to Drewville on cases where he'd been named special judge that he'd not hit the front door of the courthouse before Amos Keeler would be tugging

at him telling him how he wanted things to go here in Drew
County. How come you didn't take a change of judge?"

"We got in too late. The time had run. The local lawyer
died."

"Died?" I asked, interested.

"Don't start that kind of stuff, Don," Jake warned. "This
one was ordinary. Accidental death in a car wreck. Pretty
tragic, but I guess he just went over that bad hill you undoubtedly drove down earlier. We heard he was drinking. So
we got the file shoved up us from the insurance company and
wound up having to defend the case. It looked like we had a
shot before we got to the courthouse."

"What was the lawyer's name?"

"The one who died? Lucas—Raymond Lucas. I knew him
some and came to the bar services for him here in the courtroom. I talked to a state cop who checked it also. An accident."

"What state cop?"

"A Robert Cadwell. He works out of the local post."

"What was going on late today?" I asked. "When I looked
in, the jury was examining photos."

Jake grimaced. "Photos of a burned something or other.
Not very pretty. He let them put a dozen in. Taken from
every conceivable angle. Piece of meat and not much meat
at that. We objected, but he let them in. The jury now is
convinced that someone died. We never argued about that
and would have stipulated it. We're arguing about *who* died."

I nodded. "Can I have your files?"

"Take Sam's," Jake said. "If you lose his, then I'll still have
mine."

"What makes you think I might lose the file?" I asked
curiously. "Do I go around losing files or something?"

"Jake doesn't like the judge much," Sam said gloomily.
"Things have gone pretty badly. Maybe it's partly my fault.

You know how many blacks there are in this crazy honky town and surrounding county?"

"No."

"Zero. None. Zip. I'm both a curiosity and a bad smell. No one wants to talk to me, including our witnesses, except for the insurance people. The first day, after we were picking jury for six hours, we went out to dinner and the restaurant people didn't want to serve me."

"They can't do that."

"That's what we told them. We eventually got served, but the food was cold. Our waiter got mad when we didn't leave a tip. He followed us outside." Sam smiled sleepily. "I had to chastise him." He looked away and then back. "Since then we get our meals at drive-ins. It's like the Deep South years back." He grinned a little at Jake. "They don't like Jews much either."

"Is that all?" I asked.

"They're all related to each other. We had a heck of a time getting a jury that's not related to someone on the plaintiff's side. Cousins and nephews. In-laws. Married my stepbrother's child by his first wife. That sort of thing."

I waited, knowing somehow there was more.

"How much did they charge you for your room?" Sam asked.

"Twelve bucks and some change."

"Your room the same size as this one?"

I looked around. "I guess so."

Sam nodded at Jake. "See what I told you." He looked over at me. "They're charging us thirty-plus bucks a night."

"All right," I said. "So they're jobbing you. There has to be more than that?"

Jake shook his head. "Our witnesses haven't testified, but we have good reason to believe they'll change their stories— or most of them will. We don't know why. We've tried to call them on the phone and the companies have sent insurance

investigators out. The witnesses, or most of them, won't talk
to us." He gave me a long, testy look. "We do know the poor
widow lady and her mean-looking stepsons who filed the case
are distantly related to the local sheriff. His name's Billy Joe
House, but everyone calls him 'Brick.' He sits in the courtroom all day and listens to every word. He jangles in and out
each recess, speaking to everyone in the hall, including the
jurors. He smiles at us like he knows something we don't.
We're afraid maybe he does."

"What would that be?"

Jake looked down at the floor. "That his people are winners
and we're losers. We're going to get it stuck in us. You know
what he did the first day before we started picking a jury?"

I shook my head.

"He came around and asked us real mean if we had any
recording equipment and then checked our briefcases to
make sure we weren't telling him a lie. I think he'd have
done it rough-like, but Sam here shook hands with him and
he got smiley-polite after that."

Sam grinned at me. He had hands like satchels.

"Is the sheriff running in the upcoming election?" I asked.

"Not this time. He has two more years." Jake looked me
over. "And then we think that the people here in this motel
listen in on our telephone calls. When we called Steinmetz
and asked him to send you, we did it on a pay phone far away
from here."

"Okay. You want me to look around? You want me to check
your witnesses and see what's happening to them—why
they're changing their stories? Anything else?"

"Whatever you can find." Jake gave me a look that had a lot
of desperation in it. "Anything. Just start as if you knew
nothing."

"And all of it has to be done over this weekend?"

Jake nodded. "Plus Monday. The plaintiffs rested today.
The evidence they presented is thin, but enough to get them

to the jury. We've got two medical witnesses we can call first on Monday. I can string them out for most of the day. There's an ex-wife who didn't like Avery Benjamin and will say so and that she knows he's still alive, that he's called her on the phone and come to see her. She's pretty flaky and not worth much, a boozer. There's statements from the witnesses who claimed to have seen Avery Benjamin, but Judge Keeler has ruled those aren't admissible. It's a legal question whether they are or not."

"There's offers to prove?"

"Don't try to teach me trial law, Robak," Jake snapped. He looked angrily down at the floor and then back up at me. "You're not that good or me that bad. Sure I know about offers to prove. There may be enough in the record by the time we get done with the trial to get things reversed at the appellate level, but you never know about that. Right now we think the judge is playing politics. We're being cast as big butter-and-egg lawyers from out of town trying to keep a poor widow lady and her stepsons from collecting insurance policies during hard local times. Rank regionalism. Even if we get it reversed, the judge has gotten himself elected again in that time."

"How about his opponent? There's someone named Howard Jay running against him next month. Has anyone talked to him?"

Jake shook his head. "No reason to. How would he know anything about this case?"

"He might have an opinion as to what's going on and why it's happening."

"You talk to him then." Jake threw up his hands. "Do what you damn well please."

I smiled. "I will."

Jake shook his head, letting the beginning of an argument go. "The other side's offered us a deal. We can settle for the face value of the policies and get around the punitive damages. Our insurance companies have people watching in the courtroom. They're suddenly inclined to do it." He looked up at me and I could see he was deeply angry about the whole situation. "And I'm pretty sure the bastard named as the insured in the policy isn't dead. I'd stake a lot on it. But there's a deadline on the offer and that's Monday night. After that the offer's withdrawn."

"And so you'll stay here tonight and go back in the morning?" I asked.

"Right. Sam and I will spend a fun-filled evening going over our stuff from my file and getting ready for Monday. Then, in the morning, we'll go back to Bington and have ourselves a gala weekend." He shook his head, still angry about what was happening.

"Why not go back tonight?"

"We needed to talk to you and I'm not driving that hill or letting Sam drive it at night. That's where Lucas, the lawyer who used to represent the insurance companies, got it. The way I feel about it, we'd probably go off it too."

"I see. Anything else you know that I ought to know?" I asked, looking at both of them.

"They've had a lot of fires around here," Sam said. "The one where Avery Benjamin died was one of the first ones, but there have been a bunch of them since. Good fires. Insurance fires in houses that couldn't be sold in today's Drewville market." He shook his head. "Arson, probably."

"Arson?"

"Be careful," Jake said.

"Sure. If someone tries to set fire to me, I'll carry an emergency supply of marshmallows."

Jake stared at me and shook his head. "Someone's sure to recognize you before long. You've been in too many newspapers."

"The lawyer probably will. I'll save him until last."

They let me out their door and I walked back to my own

room. There was no moon. I wasn't sure at all about being watched. I felt like there were eyes on me. I thought I caught movement at the far end of the parking area, but when I walked there I found nothing.

I went to bed.

CHAPTER TWO

*Steinmetz's Question: "Do you want police or citizens run-
ning your world? Nine times in ten, the answer is citizens,
but the other time it's police. Wisdom is knowing which
single time."*

In the morning, by the time I awoke, my partners Jake
Bornstein and Sam King had departed for Bington. The door
to their motel room was open, and Jake's car was no longer in
front.

Outside, the sun was coming up in the east and the
weather had grown appreciably cooler overnight, maybe low
to mid-forties, but it looked as if there would be at least one
more brilliant fall day.

I put on my running clothes, which I'd packed, and went
out into the bad, but interesting world. Before I left I arranged my suitcase so that I could tell if anyone tried to go
through it while I was gone. I took a hair I found on my pillow
and threaded it through the lock until it was almost invisible.
I figured someone would eventually become interested in
me, but it was early for it now. Or maybe, remembering my
feeling of being watched the night before, it wasn't.

I hid the case file in a space between the wall and the
medicine cabinet.

Then I ran.

It's a good way to learn the layout of a new town.

The east-west streets were numbered, the north-south
streets named for trees. I ran through a cutting wind and a

few falling leaves in the early morning cool, moving easily, accustomed to the running. Running isn't for everyone. It gets to many people, pounding the gristle out from between the bones of the feet, damaging knees and ankles, but it had yet to bother me. Or I had yet to find out it was bothering me.

Twice I was passed by a town police car, an aging white Ford obviously not intended for the serious pursuit of any fleeing Drewville villains. The first time the single occupant looked me over carefully, the second time he waved and I waved back.

The northeast part of the town was the best residential area. There the "For Sale" signs were less in evidence, the houses sat on bigger lots, and the cars in the drives were more expensive. I saw two lots with blackened ruins from fires there, plus several other fire sites in the less expensive housing.

I also smelled the early morning odors of coffee brewing and bacon frying and found I was hungry for breakfast. I pushed the hunger into a remote spot inside my head and ran on.

Farther east, there was a boat-rental area where you could rent canoes or rafts for what the signs in front called a "thrilling trip down the river," or motorboats for fishing. There were eight rental buildings interspersed among the houses built along the riverbank. I ran near the edge, and the water, even at this time of the year, ran white and swift. Steinmetz would like it. He was the office fisherman.

The south part of the town was small factories, several of them now closed. The ones that looked open were a tack factory, a small tool-and-die company, and a shoe factory.

The grade school and high school were in that area also, near the Burger King and a couple of other fast-food outlets. The school buildings were new, probably constructed with bond issues when the nuclear plant was being built, brick and stone, with wide windows and a huge gymnasium for basketball. An optimistic school system which now burdened the area tax base. A sign on a fence that fronted a parking lot by the gym read: "Caution. This is the home of the dangerous Drewville Blues."

I ran on.

There was one industry of special interest to me and I ran all the way around it, one city block on each side, not far from the courthouse. The front entrance had a sign that read, "Benjamin Construction and Hardware Company." The grounds and the run-down buildings were enclosed by a rusted barbed-wire fence erected on high steel posts. Inside I could see a combination retail store and office building, plus some storage and maintenance garages. One newer building held lumber in varying sizes. There were rows of equipment parked on the gravel lot, most of it road-building vehicles. There was a paver, three earth movers, and a long row of dump trucks, plus some smaller vehicles. They all looked well used and, in some cases, worse, held together apparently by prayers and wire and glue. They were all painted bright red with a white "B" on the doors. There was no one about at this time of morning. I had my look and then kept running.

At the far edge of town I turned and came back down the main street toward the motel. I passed the trailer park. A few rusty trailers still sat among the multitudes of paved spots, looking lonely. The park was as big as half a dozen football fields joined together, but now I counted and there were only four trailers left in residence.

The shopping center was burned out. I ran into its weed-grown lot and past the foundations of a long building divided into large and small areas. Maybe intended for a chain supermarket, a drugstore, and some smaller stores. Now there were only the crumbling foundations and some blackened timbers left.

At the exit of the shopping center grounds the local police officer waited patiently in his old white Ford. He rolled his window down and beckoned. I nodded agreeably and ran his way. I stopped at the side of his car.

"Yes, sir?" I asked.

"Now, just exactly who would you be and what would you be doing?" he asked back. He had an open Irish face and he was an older man with a pronounced paunch. His eyes were harried and blue-black and his face and neck were wrinkled and creased enough to hold a winter rain. He wore sort of a uniform in that his shirt was blue and he had a gold badge pinned to it. He carried a large rusty pistol in a holster at his side. His clothes were clean, but faded. I guessed him at sixty-plus, a medium-sized man. He was chewing tobacco, so I stepped a little to the side to give him whatever room he needed.

"Name's Robak. I'm staying at the Valley Motel up the street. I run for exercise. Been doing it for years. What happened here?"

"There was a fire. Two fires, really. We've had a God's plenty of fires, way more than our fair share. That's why strangers interest me." He leaned out the window and spat accurately away from me. "Why are you in town, Mr. Robak?"

"The trial and the story behind it. Avery Benjamin."

"You a reporter?"

"Something like that," I said. "Want to see some identification?"

He nodded affably enough, relaxed now.

I got out the Brockton Publications press card and my room key from the motel. He looked at them with only cursory interest and then handed them back.

"Nice to have you with us," he said amiably. "The town can use the business."

"Where's the best place in town for breakfast?" I asked.

He shook his head. "I eat at home and I've found out it ain't good politics for me to prefer one local place over the other.

You look around and you'll find a place." He revved up the
sick engine on the Ford, listening carefully to its whining
protest.

"Doesn't look or sound like it's in the best of shape," I said.
"Did you win the car as a consolation prize in a demolition
derby?"

He shook his head gently again and smiled. "Don't be
smart-ass, Mr. Reporter. Matilda here ain't the best of cars,
but she's all we got. She uses four quarts of oil a day and we
don't like to turn the motor off for fear it won't start up again.
But no money for a new car." He sighed gustily, thinking on
that. "Not this year. Maybe not any year. So we pamper her
and insist everyone, you included, talk gentle and nice to
her."

I nodded. "I see. Nice Matilda. Okay for me to go?"

"Sure. Good to have you in town." He grinned.

"Thank you."

"Be careful of all this wild early morning traffic." He shook
his head reprovingly. "Now I'm being smart-ass."

"Did you know Avery Benjamin?" I ventured.

"It's a small town. Everyone knows everyone. A lot of folks
are related. So, sure, I knew Ave. I also know his wife, Hilda,
and his ex-wife Cherry and her two sonny boys. Used to hunt
with them all when things was cheery, before Hilda come
along. And me and Matilda here have transported Ave on
occasion."

"Is that what they called him? Ave?"

"Some did."

"Did he have a drinking problem?"

"Ave drank a bit." He nodded and smiled, showing to-
bacco-stained teeth. "Sometimes quite a bit." He looked out
his window and squirted tobacco juice. "He used to own a
chunk of this shopping center that had such bad luck."

"You said they had two fires here?"

He nodded. "Two of them. One early in construction,

when the project was maybe half up and things in town was looking sweet. Another after the nuke plant closed down. No insurance the second time."

"And Avery Benjamin owned part of it?"

"Most of it. Him and Cherry."

"I hear that some say it wasn't him that died in his home fire and others say it was."

"That's what the lawsuit's about," he admitted, solemn-faced again. "Wife one says he's alive, wife two says he's dead. The boys, standing to gain lots from it, say he's dead also. Ave got a little mad when he had his first shopping-center fire. Said they paid him twenty cents on a dollar. He got a lot of life insurance about then, I heard. Then he had another fire here and then he burned up at home. That's a lot of fires for one man."

"You have an opinion about the home fire?"

"Not me. Not my business. You seem like a nice young man, enterprising and all, but it ain't my business." He gave me a regretful, vague wave, put the car in gear and drove off in a cloud of blue, choking smoke. I watched him disappear, figuring he did have an opinion, but that I wasn't going to hear it.

I went back to the motel. The shower water was warmer in the early morning. No one had bothered my suitcase, and the file was still safely behind the medicine cabinet.

The motel room smelled faintly of whiskey, perfume, cigarettes, and old assignations.

I drove out and found an eating place downtown called Babe's that seemed full of locals, and had my orange juice and eggs and black coffee there. I listened to talk about the weather, about the possibility of the nuclear plant reopening, and about how bad business was. No one within my earshot mentioned the Benjamin trial, although I lingered over a second coffee for a long time. The conversation was peculiar for a small town. Usually in Bington, where I lived, at breakfast you'd hear laughter, insults, and the like. If a big trial was going on in Bington, there'd be talk of it. Here in Drewville, it was as if everything was moving at half-speed, subdued, as if all were watching all and living by cue cards, saying little.

A waitress fluttered around me, filling my coffee cup, asking if all was well. She was an older woman, ugly as a mud hut in a rainstorm, but good at her job. I overtipped her so she'd remember me. The eggs were fluffily basted and the whole-wheat toast buttered just right.

"You have a good day," she said when I paid at the cash register.

"I had other plans," I said, smiling.

"Oh, you," she said and lifted her hand in a mock swat.

"The breakfast was very good," I said. "I'll be back early for lunch. What's your name?"

"They call me Milly. Try to get in before the noon rush," she advised.

The district state police post was located on the winding highway that followed the river north of town, far past the bad hill road. The post seemed to be an old residence that some enterprising state police architect had remodeled into usability. Inside, a young, fresh-faced radio operator sat stiffly in a well-starched uniform behind an imposing array of equipment. A rail and a swinging half-door kept me outside of him. He eyed me quizzically.

"Is Trooper Robert Cadwell on post?"

He shook his head. "He ought to be along in a minute or two. He's due in right now if he didn't stop someplace for coffee. And it ain't Trooper, mister. It's Corporal Cadwell."

"Okay for me to wait?" I asked, unabashed.

He nodded and went back to his equipment, but it was a slack time and there was very little happening.

I waited. The minutes passed. A trooper entered and gazed at me curiously, but the radio operator shook his head at me. Finally another entered and the radio operator nodded.

Robert Cadwell was graying, fortyish, and tough-looking. He was tall, thin, sort of shambly, and there were crow's-feet lines shadowing his eyes once he took off mirror sunglasses. He wore little badges above his uniform pocket showing his years of service: five, ten, fifteen, twenty. Another badge showed he was an expert pistol marksman. Another at his collar showed he was, indeed, a corporal.

"My name's Robak, Corporal. I wonder if you'd have a few moments to speak with me?"

"What about?"

I handed him my press card and he gave it one quick look and handed it back.

"I'd like to ask you about the accident where Raymond Lucas died."

"Why would you ever want to do that?"

I shrugged and waited.

"I can get you an accident report, if that would do it?" he said neutrally. His voice was smooth. He'd dealt with the public for a lot of years and I could almost see him trying to decide just where to fit me. "You'd have to pay for it," he added.

I nodded agreement. "It could help. I'd still like to talk to you some about it."

He smiled equably. "Wait a minute." He turned his back on me and vanished into one of the rooms down the center hall. When he came back out he handed me a copy of an accident report. "That's two bucks, one buck a side, two sides. That's what the state says we charge for them, be you prince or pauper." He smiled at me and I dug out my wallet and paid.

I glanced down at the report. I'd seen them before and paid the two dollars before, usually in criminal cases. The accident had been a one-car accident. Ray Lucas had gone over the side of the bad hill. There'd been a half-empty

whiskey bottle in the front seat, a bottle of Early Times. He'd
been driving a late-model Chrysler which the report showed
as "totaled."

"Anything at all out of the ordinary about the accident?" I
asked.

He shrugged. "Nothing I could see. That's a mean hill, but
it's the only way in from that direction. Ray knew the hill. It
was just an accident." He hesitated and looked at me. "There
was one thing that was kind of odd."

"What was that?"

"Ray usually drank scotch, but maybe he just ran out that
night. I was with him at a FOP fish fry a week before and he
was sure heavy into the scotch that night."

"Anything to indicate his car might have been forced off
the road?"

"No. Nothing I could see or find. You go off the road that
high up and come down into the valley as far as Ray came
that night, turning over and over and end over end, and
there ain't a lot left to examine." He looked at me. "Did you
come down that hill?"

"Yes. When I came into town."

"Every year the state's going to reengineer it, but they
never get around to it. This is a small county here. Not
enough votes. Nobody up in the governor's office gives a
damn about Drew County. We lose one or two on that hill
every year, usually high school kids, usually high on pot or
booze." He looked me over, curious about me because I was
checking something he'd written off. "Why are you interested in what happened to Ray Lucas?" he asked again.

"He was the attorney for the insurance companies getting
sued in the trial about Avery Benjamin. While he was the
attorney, nothing much happened in the case. When he died,
things started happening. That interests me." I paused. "A
lot."

"Better not let good Sheriff House find you checking things

like that. He gets even more redheaded if anyone even talks about Avery not going to glory peacefully stoned in the fire or tries to suggest that something's wrong around here in little old Drew County. He catches a high school kid with a can of beer and makes it into a federal offense."

I nodded, not really worried about the local sheriff.

"I mean it," he said. "Mr. Macho don't like anyone fooling around asking questions in this county without his consent."

"That's too bad," I said. "Maybe I'll ask his permission, but I doubt it. If I came around sometime and asked you to show me the exact spot where Mr. Lucas went off the road, do you think you could manage that?"

He shrugged. "There's nothing to see, but I guess I could do that. You can find it yourself without trouble or me. Top of the hill. There's a tree with the side scraped off. He went down right there. You can still see the trail. All the way down." He watched me. "There's a lawyer in Bington named Robak who did a lot of criminal work. I've heard he's a mean cat to clean after. You related to him?"

"Yes."

He smiled. "I'll bet you are at that. He'd be just about your age."

"Very close relative," I admitted. "Another thing. Did you order a blood alcohol on Ray Lucas?"

"No. Maybe I would have if it had been a two-car accident, but Ray was dead, no one else was around, he had a wife and son, and was known to do a little late-night running. So I let it go." He looked at me. "Now I'm getting curious because you're curious. Maybe I should have had that done."

"Maybe. Who did he run with?"

"I don't know," he said.

I frowned.

"Ray ran with several ladies," he said. "Widow ladies, divorced ladies. I guess it don't hurt him any to say it now."

"Who?" I asked again.

"Try Cherry Benjamin. I heard he was after her, but it might have been Hilda. I didn't keep up real good on his love life. None of my business—or yours."

I couldn't think of anything else.

"Thanks for talking to me," I said and did think of something else. "What happened to the wife and son?"

"Moved upstate with her sister right after Ray died," he said. "You come back and see me later if you find any reason why I really should have done more checking. Ray and me was close personal friends."

"Sure," I said. A new thought came. "Did anyone from the post make the run to Avery Benjamin's place when he was supposed to have been burned up in the fire?"

"No. That would be the sheriff. Later I heard the state fire marshal came down also." He shook his head. "The sheriff don't like us messing around in anything but state highway stuff, not that we give much of a damn what he likes."

"That way, eh?"

He nodded. "Some of them want to run the whole thing. He's one who does. Napoleon type. You watch out for him. Sometimes I think he ain't all there." He twirled his finger near his ear.

"Has anyone else died in one of these fires you've had around here?"

"Two kids. Separate fires. Those two could have been accidental or set. One of the kids was eleven years old, the other maybe nine. Old enough to stay home while their parents were out partying in the local gin mills. Old enough for their folks to maybe buy insurance on them." He shook his head. "Both families have since moved on. Maybe the FBI could find them, but it wouldn't be easy. Migrant construction workers."

"Sounds mean."

He nodded. "I heard from the fire marshal that he thinks

most of the fires were set. He wasn't sure about them two, but he was suspicious. Wrong time of the year for flue fires."

"What's a flue fire?"

"You get them when you first start a furnace or build a fire in a grate or stove. Stuff in the chimney catches and sets fire to the roof or ceiling." He shook his head. "I ain't sure that them two fires ain't like the others—set for insurance money. When you ain't got a job it's hard to feed your kids." He shook his head. "Lots of folks turn animal."

I drove back to the Benjamin Construction Company. The big gate was open now and a few of the small trucks were gone. I parked across the street and watched for a time, but nothing happened. They seemed to sell lumber and siding from the newest building inside the compound, paint and hardware and the like from the office. I watched a few people enter, make purchases, and then drive away.

The day had grown warmer and I could smell what I thought was the odor of burning leaves coming from some-where.

There were two men running the store inside the fence. They were both thirtyish, large, and active. I wondered if they were the Benjamin brothers, Avery's sons. From the looks of the equipment I guessed they were. There didn't seem to be enough money around to hire help. Not now.

The Benjamin brothers, if that was who they were, looked tough and competent, both big men, well muscled. I thought about ways to observe them close up and finally got out of the car and walked over into the compound.

I wandered about the shed and then into the office building. Stock was sparse both places. I bought a sack of nails I could use at home and a small can of paint to paint a shelf in my garage, a job I'd put off for a long time.

The youngest one waited on me at an ancient cash register in the office building. "How's it going?" I asked casually.

He nodded, perhaps thinking he knew me. He had curious amber eyes, shaped peculiarly, almost as big up as sideways, Orphan Annie eyes. "Okay. Should go to the jury next week." He looked around the building. "You need anything else?"

"Maybe later. I'll come back when I see."

"You do that, hear?" He grinned. "We'll have us a real big jamboree-type sale when the trial's won."

"Fire sale?" I asked, smiling sympathetically.

He nodded. Something came into his amber eyes and I saw he no longer was sure about me and I wondered why. Maybe I'd gone too far. It was a Robak failing. He stopped talking, followed me to the door, and watched me suspiciously out into the street.

I opened up and put the nails and the can of paint in the trunk of the LTD and waved affably to him and he shook his head and went back inside.

I looked at my watch and it was coming on early lunch time. I drove back to Babe's and parked in front. Inside it was still semi-deserted. I sat in a booth and my waitress of the morning spied me immediately. She brought me a menu and poured me some coffee.

"What's good?" I asked.

"Try the meat loaf." She eyed me carefully. "You're new around here."

"In town for the trial." I laid out the press card and she oohed and aahed over it. I asked, "What's the inside story on what's going on around here?"

"I don't know. You hear both sides. A few people still say that Avery Benjamin's hiding out someplace laughing at the insurance companies, but they don't say it loud anymore. His boys beat up one guy used to work nuclear who said it. That guy left town. Most locals think Avery's dead; if not in the fire, then those boys of his probably killed him or he drank himself to death at his fishing and hunting cabin. No one seems to know exactly where it is other than maybe the boys and Cherry. Someplace near the river."

"I never heard about a cabin," I said.

Her lip curled. "That's all he mostly did—fish and hunt and drink and raise hell with the boys and his wife and, before her, his ex-wife, Cherry. Some people say he had a cabin down on one of the river's lost branches. Big hunters, the boys and Cherry. Hilda's into other sports. You'll hear about that." She nodded nastily. "French fries or mashed?"

"Mashed." I gave her the rest of my order. In the back I could see her talking to the cook, a small, fat man. He shook his head at her and the rest of my time in Babe's was silent time.

A cabin near the river?

CHAPTER THREE

*Trial Lawyer's Belief: "There are three versions of a fact:
(1) what actually occurred; (2) what an eye witness testifies
occurred; and (3) what the good trial lawyer makes a jury
believe occurred."*

I went back to the motel and dug out Sam's case file. I also
checked my bag. The hair was still in the lock, the bag un-
touched. My bed was carefully made and there were clean
towels in the bathroom, so it wasn't that they'd not had a
chance to prowl my room. I guessed I hadn't been noticed by
the right people yet. But I still felt, at times, that someone
was watching, someone careful and cautious, perhaps more
curious than anything else.

I sat in a chair by the window and opened the curtain and
read the file. There were seven witnesses listed on Sam's
copy of our witness list who were noted as witnesses who'd
"seen" Avery Benjamin since his "death." Some of them had
rural-route addresses, but three lived in the town of
Drewville. In addition to the seven witnesses, in a separate
paragraph, Sam had also listed an address for Cherry Benjamin, Avery's ex-wife. He'd put a big question mark after her
name, then drawn a bottle in which three X's were centered
after it. *A drinker.* Sam had no use for heavy drinkers. Except
for Steinmetz, whose Bourbon excesses were legendary.

I thought I ought to see Cherry Benjamin first.

There was nothing in the file about other fires or other
deaths resulting from those fires. I made a mental note to talk

more to Jake and Sam about them. Coming in from out of town to try a single case, they might not know about the extent of the rash of fires.

I decided to visit the three in-town names alphabetically after I saw Cherry Benjamin. I copied their names off on a piece of motel stationery and returned the file to its hiding place.

Despite the coolness of the day, Cherry Benjamin was working without a coat in the yard of her small bungalow. She was using a rake and gathering leaves and dead grass into small piles, then bagging them in plastic bags. An old, mud-spattered Jeep station wagon sat in her gravel drive. On the rear bumpers there were two new bumper stickers. The one on the left read: "Call on God." The one on the right said: "He is Coming."

She was a big woman who'd once probably been very handsome. Vestiges of it remained, but now she was sixtyish, lumpy, made up of slabs and angles instead of curves, and her gray eyes seemed tired and bewildered by life. She wore old clothes, jeans and a frayed and faded shirt. She was without discernible makeup.

She watched me park and come toward her.

"Hi," I said. "My name's Robak."

She rested on her rake and I caught the odor of her, soap and water and leaf-smoke smell. "I thought that might be who you were. You're partners with them other two. I just talked to them a couple of weeks ago." She looked around her yard and up at her inexpensive house. "I got no time for you today."

"None at all?"

She shook her head. "My boys don't much like me saying what I said about Avery, that he's alive. But on the witness stand you get sworn to tell the truth and I'll tell it true and right. Now, I got a lot of work today and I've also got church today."

"What church is that?"

"Most Holy Redeemer Church." She gave me a penetrating look. "Maybe you'd like to come with me? Strangers always welcome. Starts in an hour and will last all day."

"I'd like to, but time's short. I really wanted to ask you about Raymond Lucas."

She eyed me forlornly. "Ray's dead."

"I know that. I keep wondering why, until he got killed, this whole thing just lay quiet. Then, when he died, suddenly there's a rush to trial."

She shook her head. "I wouldn't know nothing about that. Ray represented me when I got my divorce and he did me okay. I got enough to keep me and what I give the Lord. But I work hard."

"Can you tell me anything about the case that Ray Lucas had, what it was that made him not worry about Avery being gone?"

"Where'd you hear that? About him not worrying?"

"Maybe from my partners."

Her eyes misted over. "I don't want to talk about Ray or Ave either one today. You tell your associates that I'll be there when they call and I'll tell the truth, like always. And tell them I won't be drinking." She looked up at the sky. "I'm born again. You ought to come to church with me. Do you good. Lawyers need it worse than anyone."

"That's probably right. Maybe I will sometime, but not today."

"Then get on," she said fiercely, losing patience with me. "Ain't no one to look after me and the true Lord but me. And I'm going to do it right and clean and straight. Better believe that, Mr. Robak. The past is done." Her eyes challenged me.

I didn't want to anger her so I retreated to the car and got in. She was still watching me, but when I started the motor she began to rake again in short, angry strokes.

I didn't find her attitude puzzling. She'd be testifying against her own sons. That was enough to make her edgy. And maybe she had a hangover, although that didn't jibe with her born again-testimony.

A big, strong, plain woman. I wondered about her for a minute or two. I guessed she'd gotten her divorce from Avery Benjamin before the big money had started to roll in. Or maybe she'd not known about that money.

I drove on.

The first non-family witness was a Jasper Carson. He lived on Apple Street and I had no trouble, after my familiarizing morning run, finding the house. Where Cherry Benjamin's house had been inexpensive but neat, Carson's was a worn-out shotgun-style house huddled near the factory section, two blocks from the school. The roof sagged and the gutters were rusted away. A crude sign in the front yard advertised that bait was for sale and another proclaimed that odd jobs were wanted. I parked in front. A man sat bundled up in an old topcoat rocking in an old rocker on the porch. He was old and bald and paid no attention to me until I got close to him. From the rear of the house I could hear a loud radio or phonograph playing country music.

"Better not come any closer," he said. "I got a cold and ain't got no bait for sale today."

"Are you Jasper Carson?" I asked pleasantly.

"I'm sure him. If it ain't bait, then you got to be from them damned insurance companies. I don't want to talk to no one about nothing. I'll say my piece on the stand when I'm called, but it ain't going to get said before then." He rocked some more.

I held out the press card to attempt to soothe him. "I'm just trying to get ahead of the game. Are you going to say what you said in your statement? Is that it?"

"No, sir. That statement was one damn lie after another. Them sneaky insurance people got me to say things just like they wanted them because I was into the wine and not thinking straight. They bought me wine and give it to me. But it wasn't the way I told them when I was drunk, hear? I've knowed Avery Benjamin all his life. I think I just wished him alive when I said I'd seen him down along the river." He shook his head. "It couldn't have been him. He was burned up and in his grave by then. Yes, sir—cold, burned meat." He smiled, liking the phrase he'd invented. "Cold, burned meat," he said again, nodding. He sneezed twice in my direction.

"Where was it you thought you saw him?"

He shook his head again. "Close by the nuke plant, but it wasn't him. I'm sure of that now."

"Positive sure?"

He nodded. "Now I am. Them insurance companies are trying to take the bread and butter right out of this town. They close Benjamin's and we'll have to drive twenty miles to buy a two-by-four." He looked out at me, seeing me for perhaps the first time. "I liked Ave. Him and me drank some together. He drank the hard stuff, but I'm mostly a wine drinker myself. I remember I was drinking that day I thought I saw him. That insurance guy got me drunk when I signed his statement. I sure ain't going to say it was Ave now. Neither are some others." He grinned, showing rotting teeth. "We think maybe it was nuke madness made us see him or maybe it might have been Ave's ghost."

"Nuke madness?"

"Yeah. Like at Three Mile Island."

I smiled to myself. I knew the nuclear plant had never been activiated. "Did someone tell you not to say it was Avery Benjamin?"

He shook his head violently. "No one tells me what to do or when to do it, mister. I'm my own man." His eyes watched the street, looking for something or someone. Then they went involuntarily to a corner of the front of his house and I followed them. There was a scorched spot there. It was hard to discern it because the house was old and needed paint, but there was a fire-charred spot right at the corner of the house. As if someone had started a fire and then extinguished it.

"Looks like you had yourself a little fire," I said. "With all the fires around, you were lucky your house didn't burn down like Avery Benjamin's. I hear lots of houses have. I even hear two little kids died."

He leaned forward once more. "Lucky. Sure. What with all the fires around here like you said, insurance from them corporation bloodsuckers is out of sight. Them damned companies put you in some kind of risky pool and it costs a fortune—more than a workingman can afford. I ain't got no insurance now."

"Where do you work?" I asked.

"Here and there. No place steady just now. I do what I can. I can carpenter right smart and I work tobacco spring and fall, did some stripping just last week. Things get better maybe I'll drive a truck again for the Benjamins. I used to do that." He looked me over again, not liking what he saw, not trusting me.

"You best get on now," he ordered. "I don't think you're interested in me or the town. You only care about selling papers."

"That's what my publisher pays me for. You'd know that, being a workingman for the Benjamins."

"Get," he said.

"Okay," I said, spreading my hands docilely.

He followed me with his eyes to the car and I saw him sneeze once more and then take a pencil out of his pocket and write something as I drove away, maybe my license number.

The next one on my list was a David Monkton. He lived on a better street in a better house, right at the dividing line between the best residential section of town and the houses that declined away from that section. His house was a neat ranch-type frame with a one-car garage.

I rang a doorbell, which played a medley of notes inside. In a while a woman came and opened the door cautiously. She left the chain on. She was middle-aged with snappish blue eyes and red hair going gray. She was a medium-sized woman, but she huddled herself small behind the door as if afraid that opening it would bring bad news.

"I'm looking for a Mr. Monkton." I said.

She shook her head sharply. "Not here today." Her voice was soft and good, an educated voice.

I held out the press card. "Do you know where I might find him?"

"Not today. He went fishing early and he won't be back till real late if I know him." She smiled glacially. "And I do know him. More than thirty years."

"Would you mind asking him to call me at the Valley Motel?"

She shrugged. "I'll tell him, but he won't call you or anyone else. Why don't you just wait and listen to what he says when he gets on the witness stand? This whole thing is beginning to wear people out in this town."

"Lady, I got an editor all over me. If I just wait he'll be on my back until Christmas."

"Well, I can tell you this: My Dave says now he never saw anyone who even looked like Avery Benjamin."

"I heard he gave the insurance people a statement that he did see someone who he thought was Mr. Benjamin after the time Mr. Benjamin was supposed to be dead. Did he give a statement like that?"

She looked up into the air. "There were lots of stories going around then. Dave heard them like everyone else. Half the town was whispering rumors and the other half had their ears to the whispers." She nodded. "A lot of folks who thought they saw Avery Benjamin have now had time to think about it and decided it wasn't and couldn't have been him."

"And your Dave is one of them?"

She nodded virtuously. "He certainly is."

"What's your husband do for a living?"

"He's a supervisor at the shoe factory."

"You had any fire trouble here, or have they had any at the shoe factory? I keep hearing about bad local fires. My editor told me to ask everyone about a rash of arsons and some kids who got killed in the fires."

"Those kids died because their folks went off to bars and left them alone when they shouldn't have. Everyone around here knows that. The town like to run those families out." She eyed me for a long moment and then shook her head. "I'll tell Dave you came past. Now I need to get back to what I was doing inside. The only other fire I know anything I can tell you about is the one on my stove."

The last town address was a Homer Scranton. He lived in a very large brick-and-stone house in the heart of the best section of Drewville. There was a shiny, almost new Cadillac in his drive. When I rang his door chime I heard a dog barking sharply from somewhere inside the house.

The man who came to the door was about my age, forty-five or so. He viewed my press card respectfully and invited me inside. He was medium-sized with very black hair and a neat, small mustache. He ushered me into a living room that had to be thirty feet across. There he sat me in an overstuffed chair and smiled solicitously.

"How can I help you?" he asked politely.

"You're on the witness list for the Avery Benjamin trial," I said.

He nodded. "I'll be there next week to testify. I've had some calls, but it's still like I said earlier. I saw Ave Benjamin in San Francisco two months after his funeral here. I was at Ghiradeli Square and I saw him out on the walk near the beach. I was maybe fifty feet away and I yelled. He saw me and ran." He nodded. "It was Ave sure as hell."

"Have people threatened you about testifying?"

"My wife said there were some crank calls early on. It's a sore subject and some locals think the insurance companies should have paid off a long time ago. When the calls started coming, I just started taking my wife with me during the week. We've got this house wired to the local police station. This place is made out of brick and stone and the locks are the best you can have installed. Someone tries to get in and probably they'd get caught. And it'd be hard to burn. So I'm sticking with what I said before. I've heard lots aren't."

"What do you do, Mr. Scranton?"

He smiled. "I'm in sales—I sell shoes wholesale. I sell for lots of people, including the people who run the shoe factory here. I call on trade all over the country. I live in this town because I was born here, but no one here has a thumb on me. That includes the shoe-factory people here. They don't want me to sell for them, then I'll survive with other companies that do."

"Has anyone mentioned you losing your local factory?"

He smiled some more. "Not to my face."

"You're the first person I've gotten to say they did see Avery Benjamin after his apparent death."

"There were big bunches at one time." He shook his head. "You see, if the Benjamins get the insurance money, they can pay off the bank on what they owe there, they can get new equipment for their business, they can bid again for road jobs, which Avery about closed them out on. When he died, if he died, there were a lot of people looking at him, including the federals. The locals think that if the Benjamins win it would make jobs, or that's what they're telling around. Besides, those boys are kind of mean citizens—the Benjamin boys, I mean." He gave me a shrewd look. "I think the way the town feels about it is who gets hurt if the Benjamins stick it to the insurance carriers?"

"Did anyone ask you directly to change your testimony?"

He hesitated. "Not directly."

"Indirectly?"

He smiled. "Maybe indirectly. But I don't like being told what to do and I made that plain. I guess they gave up on me thinking I couldn't hurt them much. One or two people testifying that they saw Ave won't be enough, if I'm guessing right. Not here in this town. Things got awfully poor here when the nuke plant shut down. I'll bet if someone did a before-and-after census that we're maybe five or six hundred people less now. Tough times for Drewville."

"That many people pulled out of town?"

He nodded. "Maybe more."

Outside, when I drove away from Homer Scranton's, I found out I'd picked up a follower. The car was a tan, late-model Plymouth. It was unmarked and dusty and it stayed well behind me, seemingly content just to track me. There was a large man behind the wheel. He wore a cowboy hat pushed back on his head.

I drove back to the motel and parked and entered my room. I wanted the follower to know where I was and who I was and then wanted to see what results that brought.

I sat inside the room for ten or fifteen minutes and then went back out to the LTD and got in. When I was on my way out of the motel lot I saw my follower speaking into a hand-held microphone. Sheriff's deputy, I guessed.

The addresses of the witnesses in the county were confusing. They were by route numbers, so I drove until I came to a small clump of houses where there was a filling-station-and-general-store combination. I pulled in and filled the LTD with gas and asked directions about the addresses. The man who collected the money knew some of the witnesses I asked about and he gave me directions to three of them. I wrote his directions down on a pad of paper in the LTD.

Behind me my follower stayed faithful. Now and then he'd use his radio, but mostly he seemed content to follow along, tracking me. When I pulled away from the filling station pump he made a quick entry behind me, rolled down his window, and asked a question or two while I waited for traffic to clear so I could enter the road.

The nearest county witness lived within half a mile of my gasoline stop. I found his mailbox and rutted drive and drove on in. I parked behind a shed. A big nondescript dog frisked around the car, not barking, merely excited at having a visitor. I thought he was part shepherd, part Great Dane, a handsome dog.

The witness's name was Mark Koontz and I found him at his barn after making friends with the dog. Koontz was a tall, older man in overalls and he was tinkering with a tractor motor. His face was dark from long exposure to the weather and he moved slowly and surely, his hands as delicate in handling the tractor parts as those of a skilled surgeon handling a scalpel.

He had an ill look to him, as if he'd either been sick and was recovering, or was sick now. Or, I thought, he might be a drinker. Drewville and Drew County seemed to have an abundance of them. When things go bad and people give up, they head for the nearest bar. Natural reaction. I'd been there once or twice myself. Now I drank sparingly.

"Saw you drive in," he said, his manner obliging. "Most people would have drove on because of Scout. He's friendly, but he's sure not economy-sized." He laughed. "Kind of like me. I used to be even bigger, but I've been trimmed down. How can I help you?"

I got out my trusty press card and showed it. I patted the dog, who sat on his haunches beside me, working now and then for my attention.

"Run him off if you want," Koontz said. "He's a pig for petting."

I shook my head and continued to scratch the big dog's ears absently.

"What can I tell you?"

"I'm down here to find out about Avery Benjamin and the trial. Your name was on one of the witness lists."

He nodded. "My story ain't much. It never was. Maybe I saw Ave, maybe not." He pointed around the barn. "You get tired of this farming now and then because it's so never-ending. There's always things to do on a farm. So I fish for relaxation. Doctor's orders. One evening, just when it was getting on dark, maybe two or three months after Ave's funeral, I thought I saw someone who looked like him on the other side of the river near the nuke plant. I was fishing out of a johnboat. I told some folks about it. Whoever it .was resembed Ave, walked like him, was built the same way. When them insurance boys came in here they contacted me and I told them what I seen." He shook his head. "I wasn't sure then and I ain't sure now whether it was Ave. Whoever it was took off, just vanished up the bank, when he saw me."

"Did anyone else ever ask you about it other than the insurance investigators?"

"No. I had a call or two, but I don't talk to people on the phone who won't tell me who they are. Then it just stopped. I've heard some others have had real problems, but nothing bad has happened around here except I had another dog and he got poisoned about that time. Scout won't eat except what I feed him. He don't have any momma and his poppa was a travelin' man, but he's one smart dog."

The dog picked that moment to put a friendly nose into my hand. I smiled down at him and Koontz smiled at me.

"He likes you," he said, marveling about it. "He'll let the kids wallow him around, but he ain't that much for grown folks most times."

"I get along pretty good with dogs. Sometimes I don't do that well with the rest of the world."

He smiled some more. "It ain't for publication, but I think I saw that same guy down on the river once since then."

"When was that?"

"A month-plus, maybe six weeks ago. Time gets away from me. I was fishing and there he was on the other side of the river. I came out of a little stream in my boat. He took off when he saw me just like the last time. The river ain't real wide, you know. Wider than in town, but still not much except swift and treacherous."

"Did you get a better look this last time?"

"No. About the same. Dusk. If I was Avery Benjamin and I was hiding out, I'd not come out until dusk."

"In your opinion was the person you saw either time Avery Benjamin?"

He hesitated. "Maybe. Maybe not." He looked down at the dirt floor of his barn. "I'm trying to be fair. My eyes ain't that good and I never knew Avery that well. I thought it was him both times, but I don't know that it was. That's what I'd testify to."

I shook my head. "If that's what you saw, then that's what you ought to testify about. I guess what I'm asking you is when you saw it, did you believe at the time that you were seeing Avery Benjamin?"

"I guess I did, or I'd never have said anything about it. I'd have said I saw someone who looked like Ave, not that I saw him."

Scout got to his feet and began to bark. A brown-and-tan car had pulled into the driveway, its doors resplendent with sheriff's emblems. The driver gave us one short, arrogant blast with his siren and got out.

"That's our good Sheriff House," Koontz murmured irritably. "Half man, half jackass."

CHAPTER FOUR

Steinmetz's Saying: "Calling a sheriff an 'officer of the law' can be misleading. Sheriffs are political animals. The main thing they have to do in this life is get elected again."

The man who got out of the car was shorter than me, but a third again as wide. He had a rough, weathered face and I guessed his age at less than thirty-five. He wore a big, shiny, ventilated gun in an open spring holster tied low down on his leg like an old-time gunfighter. He had a thick bush of red hair and a thin, darker mustache. He nodded at Mark Koontz and surveyed me carefully.

"We've had some calls complaining about this guy. Is he giving you some trouble, Mark?" he asked.

Koontz shook his head. "No trouble here, Brick," he said, his face solemn.

The sheriff faced me, ignoring the answer he'd gotten from Koontz. "Maybe you and me ought to get in my car and go someplace and talk between us. You been running around my county acting like something you ain't and asking a lot of questions. I don't allow none of that stuff around here."

I shook my head. "Whether you allow it or not means nothing to me. It's inside the law. I'll go with you if you place me under arrest, Sheriff. Otherwise talk here, unless Mr. Koontz wants it some other way."

"If I say you go then you'll go—believe me."

I shrugged and waited.

Koontz shook his head, his face expressionless. I knew,

from his words when the sheriff arrived, that he didn't like the man, but I didn't know why.

"You been running around bothering a lot of people," the sheriff said loudly. "This here's my county. Maybe I ought to place you under arrest at that. We can have our talk down at the jail if you don't want to cooperate and come with me civilized."

"Am I under arrest then, Sheriff?" I asked softly. "I want Mr. Koontz to hear you say those magic words. He can then testify concerning them before the nearest federal magistrate." I smiled. "I always wanted to own a small-town jail as long as it wasn't lived in by a small-time sheriff."

He shook his head irritably. "You don't understand or want to understand. I run things here. And I'll tell you when you're arrested, Mr. Wiseass Lawyer Robak."

"You do that," I said, smiling at him some more. "I'll keep listening. I see you already know my name. I wonder how?"

The sheriff turned back to Mark Koontz. "You should have sicced your big dog on him, Mark. He's part of the out-of-town crew who are in here trying to bilk poor Hilda Benjamin and Cherry's boys out of their rightful money."

Mark Koontz's eyes went back and forth between us, not as certain now.

"Now how would you know that, Sheriff?" I asked. "I came in here ostensibly to do some newspaper work. I've got a press card to prove it. I invite you to check it out because it's genuine. Sometimes I practice law, but if you checked good, you'd have found I don't do any civil cases. I'm strictly a criminal lawyer."

"You're part of the same firm that's representing those two stealing insurance companies."

I nodded. "I'm part of their firm, happy to admit it. But I don't usually involve myself in civil cases except when things are out of kilter. What I'm interested in is why you, an officer of the law, went to all the trouble to find me out. Someway or another I think I'll discover that while I'm here. Seems to me you got worse troubles than me to investigate and aren't doing much about them. Fires, for instance. Awful lot of fires around your jurisdiction."

"You bad need your slats kicked in," he answered darkly. "You're a damn out-of-town troublemaker."

"You're scaring me to death, Sheriff. Why, I'm all a-tremble."

"You need scaring. You need your slats kicked in," he said again, his voice low and angry.

"You try kicking them in and you'll love federal court, whether or not you manage to get the job done," I said just as angrily. I looked him over. He was wide, young, and strong and I figured he could take me, but the running had given me great stamina and I doubted it would be easy for him. I look like I'm big and clumsy and all elbows, but I'm not that bad. I'd stay away from his bull-like rushes as long as I could and then try him on for size when he tired.

I waited, available. People had been threatening me all my adult, legal life and I 'was still alive and curious. All that threats did was make me more curious.

The sheriff eyed me uneasily, perhaps not wanting to do anything in front of Mark Koontz.

"What was he asking you, Mark?" he asked reasonably.

Koontz gently shook his head. "Private conversation, Brick."

The sheriff's face reddened some more. "That ain't friendly, Mark. I asked you a civil question, one I've got me a right to ask. You siding with him against me?"

Mark Koontz shook his head, his voice gone cold. "You came on my land without my invitation or a call. You blew your damned siren at us for no good reason other than the fact you always were a natural-born jackass since the day you were born. You got out of your car like some kind of king and started in on someone who's my guest. I figure most of the right's with him." He nodded. "I hear them out there talking about you, Brick. They say you got yourself a Jesus complex. I used to be a commissioner in this county. I got some friends. I better not see that Jesus Christ stuff again on my property. Next time you come on without papers or invitation I'll take a twelve-gauge to you." He looked down at the ground and kicked a small hole in it with one big boot. "Now I'm telling you to get back in your damn fancy car and drive on."

The sheriff waited a long minute. Then he nodded his head. "I ain't going to forget this, Mark. The Benjamins are friends of mine and supposed to be friends of yours. I'm going to tell them boys and Hilda what you said."

I thought I heard a veiled threat in the sheriff's voice, but it didn't affect Mark Koontz.

"I ain't got anything against Hilda, Cherry, or the boys, and I kind of like, or liked, Avery." Koontz grinned. "The way I figure it this ain't exactly part of that. This is just you big-manning it on my land. We go back a long way, you and me and my dead brother. Now get off my property." He nodded. "And you better tell your side of it around because I'm sure as hell's hot going to tell mine. Let's see who folks believe, me or you."

I thought for a long moment that the sheriff was going to contest it. I thought he was going to draw the big gun at his side and order me into his car. I could see the desire to do it running through his eyes. Then he shook his head. That worried me some. He was not only mean, but he was conniving mean. I wondered what drove him and why he was so interested in me. Some of them adopt a position and stick to it. I was an interloper and he was a native. I could relate to that, but both of us knew I had a right to do what I was doing.

He went back to his car and started the motor. He rolled the window down and nodded at me. His eyes were as cold as Canadian snow.

"I'll see you again," he promised me.

I gave him my very best smile. "If we do see each other, will you buy the drinks?"

He backed away in a small shower of gravel.

"He will see you, too," Mark Koontz said. "He's apt to lie in wait for you someplace private." He shook his head. "I've known him since he was a boy. I had a brother about his age. I was the first, then my folks had three girls, then Bill come along like the tail on a kite after the rest of us was full-grown. Brick used to whomp on him every time he got a chance. Mean bastard. If he couldn't whip someone his age with his hands he'd get a club. I was too much older then to take much of a hand. Now, when age don't mean that much, I'm a bit poorly to try him." He smiled without humor. "You gave me an opportunity I been waiting for a long time. Even if you didn't come on here completely truthful, I'm for you."

"I hope it doesn't cause you any trouble," I said. "My partners came in to do the trial. One of them is the wrong religion, the other's the wrong color. No one wanted to talk to them. They thought maybe people around here might talk to me. So I got asked to come and question folks. And the newspaper did ask me to report the trial for them."

"No trouble as far as I'm concerned. But you watch yourself. You got anyone else on your list to talk to?"

I nodded. "Three more."

"I'd save them for another day. Brick or his deputy will be waiting for you out on the road. What you'd best do now is drive on out my back road. It lets out down the way a mile or so. On another road. Then get yourself back to town where's there's lots of people. You want to talk to anyone else out here, you give me the names and I'll have them meet you here tomorrow afternoon, say three o'clock."

"That'd be great." I gave him the other names I had and he wrote them down laboriously.

Mark Koontz nodded his head when I was done. "I'll have

them here tomorrow. I know them all. Come back here the same way you go off the land."

"I appreciate it."

He smiled. "I liked the way you worked Brick when you first saw him. That was real class. You ruined part of his day. Then I finished it for him. Better than any medicine the doctors are giving me."

"I hope you're right about that," I said, liking the big man.

"I'd like to fight Brick sometime if I ever get well enough. For me and for my brother. He didn't come back from Vietnam. No one knows exactly what happened to brother Bill. But my guess is he was watching us from someplace high or low and approving of the way we did it to his old buddy Brick."

"I'm peaceful myself," I said.

He eyed me. "Maybe. Maybe not. I was reading your eyes when Brick was threatening you and you didn't look scared. And Scout likes you. That's enough for me. Scout don't make mistakes. Did you notice when Brick got out of his car, Scout headed for the barn. Scout knows. You get around Brick you watch his feet. He's a great kicker, Brick is. He ain't as tough as he thinks because he ain't real quick, but he's strong and solid. Bill used to say that Brick didn't like being hit in the face. Thinks he's pretty, I guess. Brick quit picking on Bill when Bill started going for his face every time." He nodded to himself, deciding some more for me. "Brick's also a great womanizer. I hear he and Hilda Benjamin were real close long before Ave was off the scene, burned up or hiding. And Brick almost young enough to be her son." He shook his head again, grinningly scandalized. "She's something, that Hilda. So was Cherry once."

"I met Cherry," I said neutrally.

"She worked like a man to make things go for Avery and then he dumped her for Hilda. Too bad, but it happens. Some people think a marriage contract's made to be busted. I seen

Cherry at a church fair a month or so back. I heard she's off the booze. She looks good. But she's kind of crazy. Always was. Now she hangs around with people that don't doctor and don't dance out at that Redeemer Church that I hear tries to brainwash kids."

"She was working in her yard when I saw her. But she wanted me to go to church."

"They might have brainwashed you too."

He smiled and we shook hands and I was directed around his barn and to a rutted road that cut along his fence and finally exited on a county road.

The trip back to town, after using Mark Koontz's back exit, was without incident.

There was one other person I could see, hopefully without problems: Howard Jay, the candidate for circuit judge against Judge Keeler.

I found his office by driving down the main street and looking. It was near the courthouse, on the second floor above a small drugstore. I parked my car and walked up, but the door was locked. It was a small-town Saturday afternoon and I'd figured most law offices would be closed, but I'd not been certain.

I drove back to the motel. I could try calling Howard Jay from there. Or perhaps, remembering what my partners had told me about eavesdropping on their calls, I should just look up his number.

No one seemed to be posted outside the motel watching for me. I went into my room.

This time things had been tampered with. Someone had picked the simple lock and tossed their way roughly through my suitcase, not making any attempt to hide the fact they'd searched it. The hair was gone. They'd not, however, found the file behind the bathroom cabinet. I decided to take it with me now.

I found Howard Jay's home phone number and address in the large economy-sized telephone book that included information for all other towns within twenty or thirty miles of Drewville. I wrote the number and address down and left the room again.

I found a curbside phone and called. The phone rang three times and then was answered.

"Hello," a male voice said.

"Howard Jay?"

"Yes, sir."

"My name's Don Robak. I'm a lawyer from Bington. I'm in town, maybe only for the weekend, and would like to talk to you."

There was a long hesitation. "Well, I'm busy this evening. A political meeting I can't get out of."

"How about now?"

Again hesitation. "All right. I can spare a few minutes. What's it about?"

"A lot of things. Your judge, for one."

His voice got stronger and more friendly. "You come on out."

I drove the LTD out to the best section of town and found Howard Jay's house. It sat on an acre or so of wooded land. It was a ranch-style, with two-car garage attached, not a flamboyant house, but well kept. The leaves had already been raked, leaving the long green yard clean. I walked up a brick path and rang a bell.

The man who came to the door was younger and much smaller than me. He had thin blond hair and freckles and he wore a set of horn-rimmed glasses. He looked hard and competent and in good shape, like a tennis player or maybe a runner.

"Howard Jay?" I asked.

He nodded and smiled. "And I know you now. I saw and listened to you making a talk at a state bar criminal-law seminar. I'd just forgotten your name. Robak, Don Robak. From Bington." He opened the door wide. "Come in. Come in."

I went in and he took me to a comfortable room where long glass doors opened out to a patio behind the house.

"Want a drink?" he asked. "My wife's out playing bridge and we have to go to a political thing tonight, so I can't have one, but I'll fix you anything simple you want."

I shook my head. "I'd like one, but best not. Your sheriff may take it in his head to pull me over and I'd hate to have my breath smell of anything stronger than water."

"You've met our ever-happy sheriff?" he asked, grinning.

"About an hour ago. For a while it was touch and go whether I'd spend the rest of the weekend in my motel or in his jail."

"He's a nasty one," he said. "He took a nightstick to one of my clients he had in his jail. I made him pay for it in court and that's made him a bit more careful." He shook his head. "The thing about it is that I still don't think he feels what he did was wrong."

"Some of them get that way. Goes with the territory."

"What was it you wanted to see me about?"

"A couple of partners of mine are in trying a civil case with your judge presiding. They called for me earlier this week. They think they're getting the short end of the stick. The witnesses they had are turning on them and the sheriff is taking a personal interest in the outcome of the trial, wandering in and out of court, speaking to everyone."

"Avery Benjamin," he said, unsurprised.

I nodded. "Tell me what's going on if you can?"

He smiled. "I was deputy prosecutor for a time after I came back here from law school. I'm the guy who put the original heat on Avery Benjamin locally. When I did, I suddenly didn't have a job. Damon Lennon, the prosecutor, who also represents the Benjamins in your case, fired me. Some other area clients also fired me. That irritated me some. I had a friend who worked for the U.S. Attorney, so I let him have some of the information I had which I'd not yet presented to the grand jury. That got an investigation started there."

"What kind of information?"

He smiled. "Big theft from the county. Things got pretty hot for good old Ave around here. For a time I was kind of a local pariah." He shook his head wryly. "I had to change parties. I got the other party to run me for judge this year. I haven't got much of a chance, but at least I've been able to say some things that have needed saying. Openly. And the newspaper has printed some of them and written some editorials. The local powers don't like that. My old pal the prosecutor doesn't like me. I don't think I'll win the election, but I sure got them scared."

I nodded.

Howard Jay smiled. "My old party calls me a traitor, my new one calls me a convert."

"Is Avery Benjamin really dead?"

He shrugged. "I don't know. Ray Lucas didn't think so. He smiled every time I asked him about the lawsuit Hilda and Cherry's boys filed, but he wouldn't talk about it to anyone. He was a closemouthed one. I don't think he even told his wife what went on in his office. Then he died driving drunk down Cemetery Hill." He looked out at his backyard. "I can't say I find it unusual that good things aren't happening to your people in court."

"Want to help?"

He shook his head. "Not me. Not a chance. Not with the election coming on. There are some people who believe what I did was right. If I got into your trial they'd maybe change their minds and say it was for spite. I could use the fee, but it's bad politics."

I watched him. "You know, there could be some advantages."

He cocked his head questioningly.

"In a trial you can call anyone you want to and make offers to prove even where they don't allow the witness to testify."

"I know that."

"Well, I don't like getting jobbed. I don't like it when my partners get stuck in the neck. I plan to help them do something about it. I'm going to have them offer a new witness list come Monday. I'm going to put a lot of your locals on that list. Then my partners will just generally raise hell and I'll sit back and see what happens as a result."

He grinned. "I can't be your local counsel, but I'll sure give you some names who knew about Avery Benjamin and what he was doing if you'll promise not to say where they came from."

"Okay. Promise. What exactly was Avery doing?"

"Cheating on road building mostly. Avery was so crooked you could pull a wine cork with him. He'd get a contract to resurface a road. He'd resurface some of it, the worst part, but maybe all he'd do to the rest of it would be treat it a little to make it look to a casual examiner like it had been resurfaced. Then he'd pay off whoever he had to pay off. And he'd give generously to his party and to individuals in it who could help him. His problem was that some of the roads were partially funded by the federals." He nodded. "He did other things. On the county roads he short-weighted stone he sold them, overbilled them, and they paid for more than they got." He looked out the window again and sighed. "He was a real sweetie, Ave was."

"I wonder if he's really dead?"

"I don't know. I'd guess yes. Someplace Hilda's got a big chunk of the money Avery stole, you can bet on that. Maybe Cherry does, too. I don't think Hilda gives a damn about the business. I hear she never goes in it these days. She's got her fortune in Mason jars, buried maybe someplace in Avery's backyard. Or in the Bahamas or Switzerland. And Avery had to take care of Cherry to get rid of her, so she's well off, too."

"You think the Benjamin women actually have money hid out in their yards?"

"No, but it's as likely a hiding place as any other. Hilda, when she bought the new house, spent a fortune putting a fence around it. Cherry got real cautious and never spends a dime she don't have to spend. She used to be into deer hunting, now she's into some crazy church."

"I was in the Benjamin business place. Not much there now."

"That's sure and certain. Cherry's boys can take what's left and be damned. Hilda don't much care about the insurance, I'd bet, but she's greedy enough to stick around when things look as good as they do now and the money's big. If Ray Lucas was still around, I'd bet you'd find her in Rio or Honolulu instead of sitting, dressed all in black, crying crocodile tears in court."

"What did Ray Lucas know that kept the case cool until he died?" I asked again.

"I don't know. He ran after Cherry for a time—or she ran after him."

"How long a list could you give me?"

"Eight or ten people. All the county commissioners and a couple of key councilmen, the sheriff, the road superintendent for the county and for the state. A few others." His lip curled. "The local for-sale crowd."

"The sheriff?" I asked, smiling. "You did say the sheriff?"

"How do you think he got to be sheriff? I don't think he was in on any of the schemes. He's crazy, but he's funny-crazy. But I know Avery gave him a bunch of money when he was running. Maybe after, maybe before he found out that Hilda and the sheriff were sometimes bosom friends."

"Can I wait for the list?"

He nodded.

"You're sure you won't come in on the case?"

He shrugged. "I've got another, better reason not to come into it. It isn't a reason I like, but it's a reason. One of the names I'm going to give you is a cousin by marriage. Another is an uncle, same way." He waved a hand, silencing me. "I don't get on with either of them and I'd indict them in a minute as a prosecutor, but I won't take a civil case where the family could be involved. That means there's lots of cases here I can't get into. My wife's related to so many people I call the county Blood County."

"I see."

He shook his head. "Maybe yes, you see, maybe no. I got to live with my wife. It's her family members, not mine. She damn-near divorced me when I was deputy prosecutor." He smiled. "One makes allowances in a small town." He got up from his chair. "She's worth keeping. I'll make you up a list."

I waited for it. He made me take it and copy it in my own writing on another sheet and then took his sheet back and tore it into small bits and then burned them in an ashtray.

"Leave no evidence," he said wisely. "Not if you have to live with my lovely, proud wife."

At the door he shook my hand. "Luck," he said. "I'll be watching and maybe laughing."

"Let's hope there's something to laugh about," I answered.

I drove back to the motel watching behind me. No one followed. At the motel someone had hung a note on my door. It asked me to call Hilda Benjamin and supplied her phone number.

Someone had shoved another note under my door. It asked me to call Cherry Benjamin "after church" and supplied her number.

CHAPTER FIVE

Jake's Maxim: "Civil cases are like horses in a race. Some of them are champions. Others are plugs. Now and then even the worst plug will give you a good race."

I sat down on the room bed and considered the two lady Benjamin notes. I've found, in my declining years, that it pays to look gift horses in the mouth and that nothing ventured is sometimes something gained.

While I was thinking I watched out my window. At any moment the sheriff could come riding up in his gaudily painted vehicle and haul me away to his jail. The fact that I might ultimately prevail over him and his county in a federal court two or three years up the line wasn't enough to make me unapprehensive.

I wished I was back in Bington where I knew the people, where Jo and Joe, my family, were, where I knew what the future was. I felt old, tired, and burned out.

I reached in my pocket and felt my list of witnesses supplied by Howard Jay and wondered whether Jake and Sam would go for a plan I had in mind.

I sighed and used the motel room phone to call Hilda Benjamin's number. The voice that answered was soft and slightly accented. Spanish or Mexican.

"This is Don Robak. Is this Hilda Benjamin?"

"No, sir. This is Linda, Mrs. Benjamin's maid. If you'll wait for a moment, I'll find Mrs. Benjamin for you. I know she's been trying to reach you."

A maid yet. That tallied with what I'd been told about money.

Over the phone, as I waited, I could hear something. It was the roar of a truck. I looked out my window. A big eighteen-wheeler was proceeding down the almost empty street outside. I could hear it from the highway and I could hear it on my phone. I remembered what Jake and Sam had said and I deduced someone was listening to my call in the motel office. I wondered why and for whom they were listening.

I waited. The sound of the truck receded.

"Mr. Robak?" a deep female voice asked. "This is Hilda Benjamin. I'd like for you to come out to the house and see me. I think we should talk about some things that are important to both of us."

"When did you want to do that, Mrs. Benjamin?"

"How about in an hour?" she asked, her voice as smooth as old silk.

"What did you want to talk about?" I asked, just as smoothly.

"Things of interest to you and your law partners. Maybe get this whole matter settled in some mutually satisfying way."

"And where do you live, since your earlier home burned down so tragically?" I asked.

She was silent for a long moment and I thought she was deciding whether it was worth her while to exhibit anger.

"Well, since I lost my dear departed husband, bless his soul, I live now in the River subdivision. Corner of Peach and First. Colonial-style house with a fence around it."

I thought for a moment. "I can't make it in an hour, but I could be there in two hours." It would be full dark by then.

"That would be agreeable. I'll be looking for you."

I hung the phone up and sat there smiling. There seemed to be no possible way that Hilda Benjamin could have known about me without the sheriff having told her. That meant he'd gone directly to her house to report, check in, go to bed, or whatever.

But how had Cherry Benjamin known where I was staying? I thought on that. A guess, perhaps. There had to be other area motels, but then she'd known Jake and Sam were here and figured I was also.

I didn't much like the idea of going to see Hilda. If she was close enough to Sheriff House to have him report to her firsthand, then I wondered if she wasn't also close enough to him to do a bit of plotting with him. What I'd heard indicated they were extremely close friends. I was getting too old to risk abrasions, bruises, and broken bones without purpose.

I called the number for Cherry Benjamin. There was no answer. I wondered what she'd wanted and why she'd called me. Maybe for her church again. Lawyers needed saving.

I decided to drive past both Cherry's and Hilda's houses now and see what was happening.

But first I sat on the motel room bed for another minute or two. I was tired. I thought again about Jo and Joe, my family. I ought to call them from here, but knowing someone was listening on the phone interfered with the urge. I'd see Hilda Benjamin and then drive on back to Bington. Only eighty miles, but just now it seemed a lot farther.

Cherry could wait for a while unless she was in her home when I drove past. Sam or Jake could talk to her.

When I got back to Bington maybe I'd call Jake and Sam and tell them to carry on alone in this case. I could beg off and stay out and away from Drew County. That would end any chance of trouble, at least for me. I got up, got my coat, and exited into the early evening. I closed the motel room door behind me.

A voice called my name sharply. "Mr. Robak!"

It was the older lady who'd checked me into the motel. She walked toward me quickly. Her eyes were squinted down and she wore a frown as if she'd just found out I had prostitutes and/or perverts in my room.

"Mr. Robak," she said. "We find we've undercharged you for last night. We'll stay with that, but for tonight the room rent will be thirty dollars plus tax."

"I'll be checking out then," I said, smiling at her. "I'll go back in and get my bag and you can have the room."

"Well, you're past checkout time, but I suppose we can accept that." She nodded, not pleased and perhaps even surprised, but accepting it. "Ain't no other good place to stay around here."

"We'll manage somehow. My two legal partners were with you last week also," I said. "I'd assume they made reservations for next week?"

She nodded again.

I looked out at the unfinished wing of the motel. Including my car, there were maybe five vehicles in front of units. Slow night. It had been busier last night, but not a lot busier.

I stared at the innkeeper. "Cancel their reservations also."

"They'll have to cancel it themselves," she said tartly, frowning again.

I shook my head. "No. I've canceled for them. They're my partners. You've been informed. Don't expect them." I reopened the door to my room. The violated suitcase sat on the bed. I crammed things hastily into some semblance of order, got the file and put it in also and snapped the bag shut. I checked the closet and carried the suitcase back outside. The old lady still stood there watching. She shook her head and muttered to herself. I smiled some more at her.

"I wish you and your place all the good luck you deserve," I said. "I do like your phone system. Very homey. The only thing I'd complain about is that the pillows on my bed seemed warm."

"This here's a respectable place," she said, offended mightily.

"Which charges different prices for different people."

"I'm Sheriff House's second cousin," she said. "You were impolite to him. And you lawyer people are trying to make a big thing out of a simple insurance claim."

"You're also in the motel business," I answered. "You won't do a lot of good running guests off in bad times. How many times does the sheriff rent rooms from you?"

She turned away without answering and went back toward her office trying not to look out at the empty road in front of the motel. I thought maybe I'd built a little backfire for Sheriff House.

I wondered if there were other reasons for her antipathy toward us. One could be because one of my partners was black and the other was Jewish. Maybe it was also because business was bad and she believed we were available for gouging.

I left the motel room key in the door and the door open to the evening cool. I put my bag in the trunk of the LTD and proceeded away without looking back.

I drove first to the corner of Peach and First streets.

Hilda Benjamin's house was easily findable because it was the only house with a fence. It was colonial in style and it was big and showy. I drove past it once and then parked across the street and looked it over. I didn't like what I saw.

There was an electric gate. It was open now, but I thought someone in the house could close it with a switch or a signal. The fence itself was maybe eight feet high and had an upside-down V of barbed wire at the top. Once inside, only a gold-medal pole-vaulter or a man with a ladder could get back over that fence. Why did she need a fence like that?

As I watched, a handsome Mexican-looking woman came out the front door of the house. She got into an old Studebaker Lark at the back edge of the driveway and started it. She drove jerkily down the wide driveway.

After she'd exited from the gate, someone inside closed the gate. It closed quickly and smoothly. Then, after a few seconds, it slid open again.

Something cold ran down my back. I wondered if I'd seen a test run. Lure me inside and close the gate on me. Then reason with me. Leisurely.

I drove to Cherry Benjamin's place. It looked safe and there was no fence around it. The yard, as I'd earlier seen, was carefully kept and there were pots for flowers on the narrow front porch. The October cold had killed the flowers, but still the pots looked nice. I got out and knocked on the door, but no one answered. The old Jeep station wagon wasn't in the drive. I wondered why she'd called and then vanished. I walked back to the LTD.

I sat out front and cogitated for a time. If Hilda Benjamin really wanted to talk to me, then I wanted to talk to her. If she was setting me up so that Sheriff House could get me into a private place, then I wanted to do what I could to guard against that.

I thought of something. It seemed possible.

When I'd gotten my "Whopper" the night before, there'd been kids and cars around the Burger King—some of them high school kids. Loud music, maybe a little pot, a little beer. From what I'd seen of Sheriff House and his brand of rough justice in Drew County and from what I'd heard from Corporal Cadwell, I doubted that all those kids would be friendly to the sheriff.

I drove the LTD to the fast-food outlet and parked in the lot. I was hungry, but thought I'd wait awhile. The inside was medium-full, some adults, some kids of all ages. Outside bigger, older kids moved from car to car, laughing, insulting each other, drinking from plastic cups, listening to loud music. I counted. There had to be a couple of dozen high-school-age kids around the lot, visiting, socializing in the peculiar way that age group does such things now. Too young for bridge, too old for kick the can. Sometimes just the right age for trouble.

One boy caught my eye. He seemed to be kind of a leader. He was thin and tall and his hair was Indian-black. He wore a blue letter sweater with a white, block D centered in it. Some of the others wore letter sweaters also. I got out of the car and stood watching him pointedly. After a time he noticed me.

He moved close, his eyes a little narrowed. "You got problems?" he asked civilly enough. "You keep watching me. It's beginning to make me nervous."

"Are you one of the bad Drew County Blues?"

He stared hard at me. "You on something, Pops? You high?"

I shook my head. "Not just now. How'd you like to make twenty dollars for half an hour's work and put three of your buddies into the same financially rewarding situation?"

He shook his head. "Money's tight around this town. What are you? Some kind of middle-aged sex freak?"

"I'm too old for that. But I do have to go see this lady. I think she may have some company waiting for me in the place where I have to meet her. If she does, I need witnesses as to what happens. All you and your friends need to do is ride along and watch."

He examined me and the old LTD. He went around to the back of the car and took a look at my license plate.

"You're out of county," he said.

I nodded. "I'm a lawyer out of Bington. I'm in town checking on Avery Benjamin."

"Who might be waiting for you other than this lady?"

"Maybe your local sheriff. Maybe someone he sends."

"Brick? Good guy Brick." He smiled nastily. "Why, all us kids just love Sheriff Brick. Who are you visiting?"

I told him. It made him grin. Excitement came back into his eyes. "An adventure," he said. "An honest-to-God adventure. Does Brick like you?"

I shook my head. "He likes me like flowers like snow."

He nodded his head at that. "Better and better. Brick don't like lots of people. He comes around here now and then and makes our lives as miserable as he can."

"I thought he might do that. He doesn't seem like the most tolerant of peace officers."

"You just want witnesses? Sure?"

"That's all."

"Okay. I'll get you some guys. But I don't know you, so I drive your car. That way I'm in control. Anything gets out of kilter, I just drive away. You sit in front with me when we go in. The other three guys sit in back." He shook his head. "I'll get you three who don't like Brick very well. Three big ones." He nodded. "Brick beat up one of our guys, a football player who'd had a couple of beers after we won a game. He beat him up bad. Brick don't have many friends left around this part of town. We like to be places where we have a crowd just now."

I waited while he chose them. He brought me three lineman types. Each of them grinned at me and got into the back of the LTD. I passed out money from a limp billfold.

The leader drove the car unerringly to Hilda Benjamin's new house. He tooted the horn jauntily as he entered the drive.

"Take it easy," I ordered. "Park a little away so it's difficult to see anyone in the car when I get out," I said. "I'd like witnesses to be a surprise for the sheriff. You can even wait to see how I'm doing before showing yourself. That's if I get jumped."

He nodded and parked back where the Studebaker Lark had once been. I got quickly out of the car and walked to the door of the house. Behind me I heard, more than saw, the front gate slide closed. I was inside and caged. I looked apprehensively out at the gate in case anyone inside was watching.

I used an impressive knocker and let it clank heavily.

A woman came to the door.

I knew she had to be fiftyish, but she was strictly something special. I think they make a few like her every ten or twenty years just to keep men hoping they'll make more.

Her hair was auburn and lustrous. Her eyes, in the light from the door, were a deep blue, almost violet, curtained by abundant lashes, overseen by plucked brows. Her features weren't Grecian or perfect, but they were alive and they interlocked together like a cunningly constructed puzzle. She wore clothes that hadn't come from a basement rack and they fit her tightly. Her tall body was extremely good. She exuded a sort of sensuality that was, up close as I was, almost overpowering. She smelled very good, some kind of perfume I'd not smelled before, but which I wanted to smell again. I found myself grinning fatuously at her.

She smiled at me. Her teeth were white and even and looked sharp. "You're Robak. Smart Bington lawyer man. I've been hearing a lot about you. Won't you come on inside?"

I was so entranced I almost followed her. Then I shook my head. "I'd rather talk out here. That's because I'm a smart lawyer man and I just saw your gate close tight behind me."

She shook her head. "Just to keep the crowd out. It's better inside the house." She shivered entrancingly. "Warmer, too."

"Here," I said again.

She turned her head a little. Her voice hardened. "He says he wants to talk out here, Brick."

The sheriff appeared from behind her. He stood smiling at me in anticipation.

"Got you now," he said, relishing it.

I stepped two steps back on the porch. I held up my hands so that they were above my head.

"That won't do you any good now, bigmouth," he said. He stepped close to me and pushed. I went sprawling into the front yard. He followed. He kicked at me, but I was expecting it because Mark Koontz had warned me earlier. I rolled away and didn't get a lot of his boot, but I did get enough to make it sting.

I came to my feet from the roll. He was right after me. I kept my arms high, frustrating his swings. At one of the wilder ones I got through and popped him pretty good along the side of the face. At the next I got a better one into his nose. I could see blood spurt.

"Stay still," he yelled.

I got another one through to his nose. It slowed him.

He drew back frustrated, watching me, trying to figure out what to do. I saw his hand reach for the belted gun. I didn't think he was going to shoot me, just use it to batter me a bit.

I heard the slam of the LTD door. I saw my four high schoolers exit the car and move closer, watching, grinning at each other.

Brick moved his hand away from his gun and I smiled at him.

"Got you now," I said affably.

"I saw that, Sheriff," the black-haired kid said. "That man had his hands up and you pushed him, kicked him, and you were going to use your gun on him." He looked balefully at Sheriff House. "Just like you did to Bucky Eggerhart just because he'd had a beer. Then you lied about it when Bucky had his hearing in front of the judge."

The sheriff looked from them to me. "Bastard," he whispered furiously to me, so low my witnesses couldn't hear it.

"Makes two of us, Brick," I said, feeling okay. I had the red urge to go ahead and finish the fight now. Here was as good as anyplace, now as good a time. I then remembered my partners, that I was working, and that I wasn't a fighter. I regained control.

I looked up at the doorway. Hilda Benjamin stood there in the door, her mouth open, somehow enjoying things even though they'd not gone all her way.

"Open the gate, lady," I said. "You don't really want to talk."

"Wait a minute," she said. "I did want to talk to you, but Brick came and he—well, he doesn't like you much. He said you were sticking your nose where it wasn't supposed to be. And he said you were a wimp lawyer. You're not."

I shook my head. "Open the gate. No talk. Not tonight, anyway."

The sheriff looked at her. I wondered who was boss. He was maybe twenty years younger than she was, and he had the power, but maybe she was running things.

She vanished beyond the door. In a few seconds the gate slid open.

I nodded at Sheriff House. "I told you I'd see you in court and now I will."

He shook his head, not particularly afraid. I guessed he'd been sued before. "You kids better watch this guy. He's part of the bunch trying to keep Mrs. Benjamin from getting her insurance money."

"They know that," I said. "And she'll get it if she deserves it," I said evenly. "You're part of the bunch trying to make sure she gets it right or wrong. What you've been trying to do is put the arm on things around here, change the odds. Now maybe they'll change back."

He shook his head. "File your lawsuit, Robak. That'll keep you busy hanging around the federal court and out of my county."

"It won't. I'll be back. I was going to leave things to my partners, but no way now. I'll be sticking my nose into things around here until they turn out right."

He eyed me with unconcealed hate and I wondered if our course had been run. Perhaps there'd be another time. I walked to the LTD and got in the passenger side. The three linemen got in the back of the car silently. They were smiling at each other. The black-haired kid rolled his window down.

He grinned insolently out at the sheriff as we drove down the driveway.

"You ain't so tough," he said. "Bucky could have took you if you'd fought fair."

Back at Burger King he shook my hand and told me his name was Ted Powers. He conferred gravely with the linemen and they offered to give me back my money.

"Like kind of a reward for punching Sheriff House in the snoot," he said. "You made it bleed and he quit cold and went for his gun."

I declined the money, which brightened their eyes.

"I'll try to catch up with you all again," I said solemnly. "I may need some more help. To find a lost fishing and hunting shack down on the Blue. Maybe to watch a church for me."

They nodded, interested.

Ted Powers said, "You ain't stopped Brick, mister. He'll be back after you again." He shook his head. "Watch your back. You done pretty good and so next time he won't give you a chance."

I nodded. "I think you're right. But you helped tonight." I gave him my card. "Anything funny happens to me you get in touch with my partners."

I left them there. I got into the LTD and drove north to an interstate twenty miles away. There, at a chain motel, user-friendly with my credit card and equipped with ice machines and color television and an empty swimming pool, I made reservations for Sunday night for Jake and Sam and myself. When that was done I used their pay phone and tried to call the number Cherry Benjamin had supplied me, but there was still no answer. Church, I decided.

Then, not going back through Drew County again, I drove home to Bington.

I spent Saturday night and Sunday morning in my own home playing with my little boy, Joe, and my little boy's mother. Fortunately Jo didn't notice the abrasion on my hip where Brick's boot had grazed me. That took some maneuvering, but I accomplished it. Snake Robak.

Sunday afternoon I drove north again.

CHAPTER SIX

Proposed Final Instruction: "In civil actions the plaintiff must only prove that what he alleges is more likely true than not true."

At three o'clock on Sunday afternoon I drove down a solitary back road in Drew County and into the rear entrance to Mark Koontz's farm. The day was cool and crisp, occasionally sunny, but mostly cloudy. I could, for the first time, smell winter coming. Only the unwary or foolhardy still appeared to have crops still unharvested in the field.

There were two rusty pickup trucks and an old brown Chevrolet four-door parked in the driveway. I parked behind them. Scout, Koontz's big dog, barked me a greeting, and came looking for a pat and a scratch and I obliged him.

I'd sent Jake and Sam on to the motel, figuring that we might fare better here with me alone than with the three of us. Drew County was Drew County.

Jake and Sam were mulling over my idea about subpoenas, liking it at times, finding fault with it at others. I planned to make one more pitch for it when I got back to the motel.

They'd known some about other fires, but it had been vague knowledge. Jake, in particular, seemed intrigued that the Benjamin fire might be one of a string of fires, perhaps done for profit.

I walked on up to the Koontz front door and stamped the driveway dust off my feet on the worn mat there. The house was old and needed a new coat of paint. I knocked.

Mark came to the door and took me inside. He had three men seated waiting in a parlor, obviously uncomfortable sitting on antique furniture. The curtains were worn and he'd drawn them. From another room I could hear female voices.

"That's wives," the first man I met said. "My wife came along and so did Ed's here. Ed's wife is second cousins to Mark. Hell, I'm cousins to Mark. Whole damn county's interrelated. The women are back there fixing coffee and warming up some stuff." He shook his head about that. "My name's Howard Leatherman. Ed here is Ed Bechtler. The silent man over on the couch is Chick Estleman. He's a bachelor. See how happy and carefree he looks?"

I looked at Estleman. He didn't look very happy to me.

"Did Mark tell you anything about why I wanted to talk to you?"

Leatherman nodded. "He said you wanted to ask us about seeing Avery Benjamin after the date he was supposed to have died." He nodded. "I think I seen him. I wasn't going to say so in court, but now I guess maybe I will. Mark here told us about how you pulled the sheriff's tail. That tickled us."

"You'll get your barns burned down," Chick Estleman said sourly from the couch. "Someone around this vicinity is burning things. I got a call, you people got calls. I don't think our caller was kidding, not with all these damned fires we've had hereabouts."

"People threatened you not to testify?" I asked.

"Someone on the phone, anonymous-like," Leatherman said. He was thin and weathered, all string and gristle, worn down juiceless by the land he tilled. He had wise eyes and I guessed him to be in his sixties, older than the other two. "I got insurance. Someone burns my place, I'll build it back better."

"If you're alive," Estleman said. He was a tiny man with an absurd and lonely face. He smiled, changing it for the better.

"But if both you guys will testify, then I will also. Only thing is I'll be scared all the time I'm doing it."

"Midge don't want me to," Ed Bechtler said. He shook his head. "And God knows them Benjamin boys are worrisome. I don't want them mad at me. I trade there some. Besides that, they're mean bastards." He sighed and shook his head. "But if Mark says I testify, then I testify. And I'll testify to the truth."

"When and where did you see Avery Benjamin?" I asked Bechtler, studying him. He was the largest of the three, not fat but stout, with great, strong arms, built like a tree. I doubted anyone worried him much physically. He wore bib overalls even though it was Sunday.

"I saw him up around Plattsburg, if you know where that is. Forty miles from here. There's a farm auction there on Friday nights. Lots of stuff for sale and a lot of people go. I went to Ave's funeral and then saw him up there at Plattsburg two Fridays thereafter. He seen me too and moved off. I tried to catch up to him, but he was long gone by the time I got out into the parking lot. I think he drove off in an old Ford truck. Ave always did favor Fords." He nodded his head convincingly. "I'm not dead sure it was him, but I think it was. Looked like him, walked like him. And run when he saw me a-watchin' him."

"Would you testify it was him?"

"Yep. In my opinion it was Avery Benjamin."

"Did you get the plate number on the truck?"

"Didn't think to do it until it was too damned late."

"How about you, Mr. Estleman?"

"I was up around Jewell City looking over a farm up there for a man I know who was thinking on buying it. I saw Ave come out of a bar across from the courthouse. I yelled at him. I've known him all my life. It was two months after he was supposed to be dead and buried." He shook his head. "I thought for a while it was maybe just someone who looked

like him, but when I yelled he took off." He smiled. "Ran like
Avery Benjamin too. It was him all right. I went into the bar
and asked about him, but no one knew him in there. Jewell
City is maybe a hundred miles north of Drewville. I asked
around and someone told me that's where Hilda Benjamin
come from."

I digested that, thinking it might come in handy.

"And you, Mr. Leatherman?"

He shook his head. "I'm not as much good as these other
two. I was with Mark here fishing in his boat. We seen Ave
across the river, down by the narrows. Mark wasn't sure who
it was, but I was. My eyes is better than Mark's. Better fisherman, too." He grinned at Mark.

"Tell me more about the phone calls?"

Leatherman shook his head. "What'd happen is that you'd
get a call. The caller would say that Avery Benjamin was dead
and that everyone knew it and that anyone who said he
wasn't ought to be run out of Drew County. Then the caller
would hang up. Some people got more than one call. Second
time the caller would say 'burned out' instead of 'run out.'"

"I got three," Estleman bragged. "Got the first one two
nights after I saw Ave." He smiled his elfin smile at me.
"When I kept saying I'd seen Ave up at the Jewell City
courthouse I got another and then another. So I shut up. And
I don't like telling it now, but I will because Mark says it's
right." He shook his head. "I'm related to the Benjamins
too."

Koontz sat like a stone man in an old rocker, listening.

I nodded at him. "Maybe the four of you won't have to
testify," I said. "I imagine you will, but maybe not. We'll see."

Koontz's eyes came alive. Sitting, I could see that he was ill.
It hadn't been that easy to tell yesterday. Yesterday he'd been
bundled against the cold. Today he seemed thin, a big man
slowly losing flesh to an unseen but known enemy, fighting
all the way.

"What are you doing that'd make it so we wouldn't have to testify?" he asked curiously.

"It wouldn't exactly be me, Mark. It'd be my partners making the decision. I've been digging around some. I gave them some names to call as witnesses. Those names aren't on our witness list, and there's no way the judge will let them testify. But we'll get their testimony in the record one way or the other—offers to prove. Legal stuff. It'll worry some of your local officials like the sheriff. We think maybe it'll change things around—that the Benjamins might back off. Stuff about the trouble that Avery Benjamin was into when he took off."

"You won't get the Benjamin boys to dismiss without money," he said sagely. "No way."

"You're probably right. You know them better than I do. If they don't, then we'll call you then. What I'll do is take telephone numbers where I can reach you people. If worst comes to worst, we'll call you as witnesses. But we'll do it last, after we try the rest, after I do my best to see if Avery Benjamin is still hiding someplace around here. If he was alive after the fire, chances are he's alive now."

"Try around the nuke plant," Howard Leatherman said. "Ave used to fish there a lot. If he's got a place he's hiding in this county, it might be down there someplace by the river." He shook his head. "Be hard to find even for someone from here who knows the ground. It's hilly and rocky with lots of trees and heavy growth. You can easy get lost back there." He looked me over. "You'd need to get some help to look."

"I was thinking about getting a lot of it." I thought of something else. "How do they start these fires?"

Mark Koontz looked warily out his window. Scout was barking, but in a moment he stopped. "Squirrel," he said. "If it'd been someone around here who ought not be around, he'd still have been going." He looked back at me. "I'm not sure. I've heard some kind of infernal device and gasoline.

Start it with kerosene, but then use a lot of gasoline. Scads of it. Makes for a hot fire." He looked down at the floor. "Little kids died, two of them."

I left by Koontz's back road and drove into Drewville. It was a Sunday afternoon and traffic was sparse. The town was quiet and shivering in the late October cold. Tomorrow would be the end of October and a week from Tuesday would be election.

I found the police chief parked, motor running, along the Blue where the boat docks were. I pulled up beside him. He had a brown paper sack on the seat and he was munching a sandwich. It looked like bologna and cheese.

He nodded at me affably.

"How's the reporting or whatever?" he asked, rolling down his window a bit.

"Could I talk to you for a while?"

"Okay. Come around and get in."

I left my (or actually Jo's) car and sat in the passenger seat of his car. The old motor ran on, making rumbling sounds.

"Still holding up?" I asked, patting the car seat.

He nodded and waited.

"I had a run-in with your sheriff yesterday."

"I heard about that. I'm old pals with Mark Koontz." He held out a hand. "My name's Evan Tucker, but everyone calls me Chief."

"I wonder if Sheriff House realizes that I've a right to investigate what's been going on here without interference from him?"

He smiled and took another bite of sandwich. I got the smell and it was bologna and cheese.

"I doubt it means a thing to him. You got to know Brick, Mr. Robak." He gave me a keen glance. "That is your name, ain't it?"

I nodded.

"Well, let me tell you some about Brick. He's mean and he's not too smart, but I don't figure he's real dishonest. The last two sheriffs we had was. Brick got brought up poor. All he knew when he was a kid was bad food and constant fighting. His pop was an alcoholic who beat his mother 'most every night. Five kids. Brick was a nothing until he found out about football. He played here and then at a small college for one year till he flunked out." He grinned. "Found out about girls about the same time and that he could either sweet-talk them or bully them into back seats. That's what he does best and what Hilda does best is done in back seats also. Two of a kind."

"How does she get along with her stepsons?"

"Middlin'. Only middlin'. Those boys are mean. They'd be a lot closer to their own mother than to Hilda. But Hilda's got the sheriff and so they don't bother her much. Brick's kind of crazy and no one fools with him." He smiled. "Except you."

"So Hilda and the sheriff are a steady twosome. Were they one when Avery Benjamin was on the scene?"

"Yep. Not as much as now, but they were sneaking and I'd guess Ave knew about it. Maybe when you get to be his age and mine, you don't care so much." He shook his head. "My bet is that Brick would never kill anyone for gain. And he's been married a couple of times and was married to his number two when Hilda came into the picture."

"Where'd Hilda come from?"

"North of here. Town called Jewell City." He shook his head slowly. "Ain't she something else?"

"She's that." I thought for a minute. "I've got one of the other lawyers in my town preparing a lawsuit against the county and against the sheriff, but I'm not going to file it until this lawsuit's over."

He nodded, his eyes reserved. "I heard from the kids what happened, but the county ain't got no money and Brick don't have any either. If you're doing it you're doing it for the principle."

"That's not the way it works. I get a judgment against the county and it makes all kinds of problems."

"I didn't know that," he answered gravely.

"I don't think he ought to be chasing around after me interfering in something I've got a right to do."

"I agree, but I won't be your peacemaker. Brick don't believe you should be doing what you're doing."

"I've got the right to do it," I repeated.

"Granted. Brick believes he's got the duty to stop you any way he legally can. And the law here is his law, not yours, Mr. Lawyer-Reporter."

"Where does that leave us?"

He shrugged. "It don't leave us anyplace. It leaves you right where you was."

I drove back to the motel and met with Jake and Sam. We sat in the central room of a suite we'd rented. It had the big center room and four bedrooms that opened off it. One more bedroom than we needed, but they didn't have any suites with three bedrooms. At this slack time of year it was only half-again more expensive than what we'd have collectively had to pay in Drewville.

Jake heard me through. The longer I talked, the more he smiled.

"What it boils down to," he said, "is that we now have five witnesses who'll testify they saw Avery Benjamin after the time of his alleged death. That's in addition to Cherry Benjamin. That's enough for the insurance companies. They'll take a chance with our medical evidence and six witnesses."

"And the witnesses who changed their stories?"

"We'll just not call them. If the other side does, then we can impeach them on cross."

"Do you want to do the other?" I asked.

He frowned. "You mean call local officials and try to ask them questions about what legal trouble Avery Benjamin was involved in at the time he disappeared?"

I nodded.

"I don't know, Don. Now that we have some witnesses, is it a good idea?"

"My guess is yes, but it's your case, Jake, yours and Sam's. I think if you do it you'll cause chaos and hard feelings in the enemy camp, you'll get the judge madder than hell in an election year, and things will just generally happen which will be of benefit to your case."

"What things?"

"Hard to tell. The word around is that Hilda Benjamin has hidden bucks and doesn't care much about our insurance case. If it gets warm maybe she'll dismiss her part. I also figure the longer you keep the Benjamins in court, the more likely Avery Benjamin is to get antsy about what's happening, maybe antsy enough to try to find out what's happening. Assuming he's still alive—now."

"Judge Keeler isn't going to let us get any of this stuff you got about local corruption before that jury," Jake said reasonably.

"I agree. But the jury will wonder about what's going on. Even if they're not supposed to know, some of the jury may find out what they're not hearing. Against the rules, but it'll still happen. Keeler hasn't sequestered them." I shook my head. "I think with your medical testimony and your six witnesses who claim to have seen Avery after the date of his death, you've got a chance. I believe if you start serving subpoenas on the local power structure, you've got a real shot. I think if you ask them questions about crooked road deals and maybe some about these other fires, your odds will improve even more."

Jake looked at Sam.

Sam nodded. "That mean judge is sure going to get awful

mad at us, Jake. And instigator Don, he won't be a part of it. He'll be an innocent come to see his partners try a case."

I grinned.

Jake thought for a long time. Finally he also nodded. "I didn't think I'd go for this, but those people in that courtroom and in this town have made me damned mad." He nodded at the room telephone. "The two of you sit right here. I'm going to call the insurance people like I promised them I would. I'm going to tell them what we've got and that we hope to get even more." He eyed me. "You are going to stay around Drewville and look around some more, Don?"

"I guess I wouldn't miss it," I said carefully. "With the way that sheriff hates me, leaving would sort of be like giving up measles and mumps." I thought of something. "How about subpoenas? The clerk might refuse to issue them to you if there's any suspicion of what they're going to be used for."

He shook his head. "I've got plenty of blank ones already signed by the clerk. Got them out of Ray's files when we picked up the case. I'll send Sam out to serve them." He smiled at Sam. "I'll have him serve the sheriff first. I can get by alone in the courtroom until he serves all of them."

Sam nodded at both of us, game.

"How about Cherry Benjamin?" I asked. "Why would she be calling me? How would she have known about me? She knew me first time she saw me when I went to her house. I think she's been in church ever since. And I don't think she's drinking."

"I don't know. Only thing I can think of for sure is that Drewville's a small town. We've got her on tap to testify tomorrow," Jake said. "I'm glad to hear you say she's not drinking."

"Better check her before you call her if you can," I said. "Those are her boys who stand to benefit from the insurance. And I didn't get good vibrations from her. One can't automatically trust someone because she says she's born again."

Jake frowned. "She's like a smoke ring. I'll probably just have to put her on and take my chances. You got anything else you need to tell us about?" he asked me. "I mean before I call."

One thing had been running around in my head, but knowing Jake I decided against telling him much about it, but a little bit wouldn't hurt.

"I've got an idea about stirring things up even more, but maybe you wouldn't want to know about it."

He stared at me, perhaps not liking the answer. When I failed to elaborate, he went to the phone and began to call insurance people.

I waited until I could hear the soft burr of Sam's snores and Jake breathing heavily. I eased out of my bedroom and then out of the motel room, closing the door behind me gently.

Figuring the sheriff and his people now knew my LTD, I'd borrowed Jo's Plymouth. Soon they'd probably also know it, but tonight it was just another nondescript vehicle with a muddy license tag. I'd muddied the tag myself.

I drove the twenty miles to Drewville and parked the car on a side street between two other cars. I was a block from Hilda Benjamin's big house.

The night was dark and the moon was down. The wind soughed through trees and I walked briskly in the cold. Winter was coming, and soon. I could feel it in my bones.

Hilda Benjamin's gate was closed. I looked at my watch and saw it was almost midnight. I walked around the perimeter of her big yard as best I could, cutting through a cross alley on one side and a back one on the rear of the house. The house appeared to be dark inside. Hilda was asleep or away. *Or maybe inside watching and waiting for me.*

Once I heard a car in the street and saw the old police car pass by, driving slowly. Whoever was driving went past without seeing me standing behind the bush of a neighboring house.

The fence was solid steel, meanly barbed, and almost brand-new. There seemed to be no way for a time. Impregnable. Then, in the prowling in the back alley, I saw that a neighbor's garage was crowded near the fence at a corner. I walked there, alert to all sounds, and looked things over. A dog barked and I stopped moving, but the barking soon ceased.

I could go up the door of the garage to the roof and then drop down into Hilda Benjamin's yard.

I looked about inside the garage. It was empty except for the neighbor's three-year-old Lincoln and some small garden tools. There was a garden hose and I thought I could tie it to something and go up and down it to Hilda's yard. But I might have to leave in a hurry and I was no longer that good at climbing. Besides, getting me down into the yard wasn't the end of it.

The hose could get me down, but not quickly up. I decided I needed a ladder and a spade for the job I planned. I had neither with me now. Next time I'd bring them with me. *When the time was right and just before the Benjamins saw it wasn't going to be easy.*

I was back inside Jo's car and ready to start it when I saw another car coming toward where I was parked. I hunched down and watched. The car passed mine without hesitating. It had gum-ball flashers on the top and a bright emblem on the door. I watched it stop for a moment while the electric gate slid silently open. The car parked in front and two people got out of it. One was bulky and shorter than me. Sheriff House. The other person who got out was female. I heard her silken, provocative laughter faintly in the night. Fifty-plus-year-old sexpot, but as real a one as I'd ever seen.

They entered the front door of the house. Lights went on and off again in the house. I was glad I'd not decided to use

the hose and some of the garden tools for my idea. I'd probably have been caught. Sheriff House would have enjoyed
that. I doubted I would.

I waited for a time, until I became certain they were
asleep, and then I drove north out of Drewville and back to
my motel.

Jake and Sam still slept the sleep of the righteous. I un-
dressed and got into my own bed and plotted against tomorrow. Tomorrow they'd serve subpoenas on the local power
structure from the list I'd been supplied by Howard Jay,
Judge Keeler's election opponent. That was bound to start
problems.

I figured I could buy my spade and a light ladder early in
the morning at Benjamin's. It seemed a likely place to buy it.
Public, too.

Tomorrow.

CHAPTER SEVEN

Lawyer's Ancient Joke: "Reciprocity is when you get one of your clients to sue one of mine and then I get one of mine to sue one of yours."

In the morning, because, if it was possible, I still wanted to keep my wife Jo's car anonymous, I followed Jake and Sam to Drewville. Jake was driving his almost-new Buick. At the edge of the city I parked Jo's Plymouth along the highway where a number of other cars were parked, probably a pull-off place from where riders commuted to the nearby cities and their jobs.

The weather was still cold. I'd worn a lined raincoat back from Bington and now wished I'd gotten out a winter coat instead. I looked up at the gray-black sky when I walked from Jo's car to the shiny Buick. Sometime soon I thought it would snow. The old line of war scars on my chest ached and that was usually a sure indication of a weather change.

I rode to the courthouse with Jake and Sam. We'd worked everything out the night before, so the ride was silent, except for Jake bragging on his new car and demonstrating its gadgets. I'm not much into new cars. You brag on them until they break down and then you raise hell because they do the normal thing. Both of my partners smiled when I ventured that opinion and were still smiling when we arrived. We parked in a parking lot near the courthouse and I could almost feel eyes upon us.

"Get those smiles off your faces before you get out of the

car," I advised. "The longer the other side thinks you're weaponless, the worse the impact on them will be. And we're a long way from winning this case. The opposition has everything going for it. Most of the people in this town and on the jury want them to win." I thought of the little old lady at the motel who'd wanted to overcharge me. "Or they're kin to somebody who is interested."

"I picked that jury," Jake said with authority. "It'll treat us fair."

"Okay. Maybe it will. But there's no need to look cheerful until the jury does what you say it will."

"Right," Jake said agreeably. "I guess maybe it's that we're so much better off now than we were Friday." He gave me a quick look as if he was trying to assess my worth. "You're useful at times, Don, much as I hate to admit it."

"You wouldn't treat me this good if I wasn't a gone-by-the-wayside Presbyterian," I said.

That got a minor glance and a short laugh. Jake liked jokes that had to do with religion. He was a constant fount of them and had no qualms telling them about any sect or creed.

We were early enough so that I could claim a seat near the front of the courtroom.

At nine a bored bailiff came into the ancient courtroom and announced, "Oyez, oyez, this court is now in session, the honorable Judge Amos B. Keeler presiding. All rise."

Amos Keeler came out wearing his black robe and took the bench. He looked around the courtroom idly, very much at home there. His eyes noted Sam's absence and I saw him nod as if something about that pleased him. Maybe he was a bigot. Drewville would be an easy town to be a practicing bigot. I ought to have Jake mail him anonymous jokes.

"Be seated," he ordered. "Counsel will approach the bench." He looked boredly out at the courtroom crowd. His eyes found mine and he nodded. *Somehow he knew me.*

Jake got up, as did his counterpart, the sallow man in his

forties, Damon Lennon. I saw Jake hand the judge and opposing counsel a list, which I assumed was the list of new witnesses.

"These people weren't on your final witness list," the judge said loudly enough for me to hear, his face reddening. He examined the list, which, I knew, having done the work to obtain it, contained the names of most of the politicians in town: sheriff, commissioners, some county councilmen, and the state and county road supervisors.

Judge Keeler looked out at me again. I smiled.

"It's been brought to our attention this weekend that these people might know something about the disappearance of Avery Benjamin and the reasons therefor, Judge Keeler. If opposing counsel objects, then perhaps a short continuance?" Jake offered smoothly.

The sallow lawyer smiled. His voice was like gravel in a hopper. "No continuances, Judge Keeler. And we'll agree to no new witnesses at this stage of the proceedings. I'm sure counsel as eminent as Jacob Bornstein and his learned associates, and all of them, know the rules of procedure."

Judge Keeler nodded, the red in his neck receding a bit. "You're right, Mr. Lennon." He shook his head at Jake. "We'll have no additions to the witness list at this stage of the proceedings, Mr. Bornstein."

Jake smiled. "As you rule, Judge Keeler. We will want to call these people and make offers to prove. And my co-counsel and I also will want to be sworn when that's done to testify for the record that we found this new evidence only this weekend."

"You mean you're going to tax the record by calling witnesses you know can't and won't be allowed to testify?" Judge Keeler asked, color returning.

"Yes, sir. They're being subpoenaed now."

"I find your tactics highly unusual and your conduct questionable," Keeler continued. "I know what you're trying to get at, but this is not the place to decide if Avery Benjamin committed some sort of criminal acts. The matter before this court and jury is whether or not he's dead. That seems a simple-enough fact situation to me."

"Nevertheless . . ." Jake began.

Judge Keeler leaned forward. "No neverthelesses, Mr. Bornstein. You'll not call these people. I'll order the clerk to issue you no subpoenas." He shook his head, a wounded fighter. "It's too late to change this case into something else."

"They're already being subpoenaed," Jake said. "We had sufficient signed subpoenas from your clerk given to Mr. Lucas at a prior time to serve them all. And, as I said, that's now being done by my co-counsel."

"Then I'll not allow them to be called."

Jake smiled. "As you please. As long as the record indicates that refusal. We're talking about felonies here. We may be talking about some arsons. Perhaps a whole string of them. In two of them children died."

I could almost see Keeler thinking. He didn't like what was happening, but if he went too far, he might put something definitely reversible appellate-wise into the record. I doubted that bothered him a lot, but it was something to guard against. "And when did you plan to call these people?" he asked, still angry, but under control again.

Jake pretended to check his list.

I looked around while there was a pause. The people in the courtroom around me were as interested in the conversation at the bench as I was. Here and there I could see people whispering together, some smiling, some frowning.

"For tomorrow," Jake answered. "For today we have an investigator from one of the insurance companies and some medical and dental testimony. And we have Cherry Benjamin." Jake looked at his watch, feigning boredom. It was an attitude I'd seen him adopt before. He was not without guile and he was good in the courtroom. "If we can get started soon, perhaps we can finish with all those matters today."

"And then you'll call these people who aren't on your list— is that it? Then will you be done?" the judge asked, his face set in long-suffering lines.

"Perhaps. We'll decide at the time. We have some other witnesses who were on the original list. We may try to call them." He smiled. "However, we find that a lot of them have changed their stories since Mr. Lucas originally took statements from them. We may want to get into that."

Lennon shook his head and started to say something. Judge Keeler stopped him by raising his hand.

The judge gave Jake a stern look. "I've already ruled that out-of-court statements can't be used to impeach witnesses you call. They're your witnesses, Mr. Bornstein. If you call them, you're stuck with what they say. I'll let you introduce their prior statements into evidence, but the jury won't see them. You can't make a case out of prior statements which differ from what's said in this courtroom. What you're laying yourself open for is a directed verdict, Mr. Bornstein."

Jake shrugged. "I heard the court's ruling. I respectfully disagree with it. I still must make the offer for the record."

I smiled inwardly. We'd agreed last night that if and when we called the witnesses who'd seen Avery Benjamin after he died, their testimony should come as a surprise, just as we'd been surprised to find that testimony changed when the trial began. It was possible that the sheriff and the Benjamins knew we'd gotten testimony anew, but finding it out was up to them. We had no intention of tipping them to the fact. And we doubted that we had—yet. Calling the local politicians was as much indirection and smoke screen as it was an attempt to pressure the opposition.

Lennon smiled nicely at Jake and both lawyers went back to their seats. I sat on the hard bench of the courtroom and watched Lennon. He seemed confident and sure. I knew nothing of him other than that he was the county prosecutor, an office of great, but not infinite power, and that he'd fired Howard Jay, Keeler's opponent, when Jay had caused waves. Lennon was, as most small-town prosecutors were, part-time, or he'd not be here trying this lawsuit. For now, in court, he looked like the cat who'd found the source of the cream. He was loving this case and his manner seemed completely confident. There was a great deal of money involved and I wondered what his contingency fee was. Fat, I supposed.

"Are we ready?" Judge Keeler asked.

"Let me get my client," Lennon said unctuously. "She's reading in the hall."

I watched as he left and returned with Hilda Benjamin. She wore a black dress and no lipstick. She had her hair in a tight bun and was holding a Bible. When I'd met her at her door, she'd carried herself proudly. Now she was stooped and old-looking, prim and proper in a dress several sizes too large for her that looked as if it had come from a Salvation Army thrift store. I almost laughed aloud.

She saw me sitting in the front of the courtroom and that straightened her up a little. She whispered something quickly and nervously to her lawyer. He looked me over carefully, but I studiously ignored him. I wondered how it was he didn't know me and yet Judge Keeler did.

I looked around the courtroom for Sheriff Brick House, but he wasn't around, not yet anyway.

There was also no sign of the Benjamin sons. I decided that good trial tactics might be to keep them out of the courtroom except when they testified. And Lennon was a tactician. Hilda Benjamin's appearance proved that.

Our first witness was a clinical pathologist from the state university. He appeared when his name was called, took the oath and the stand.

Jake qualified him by asking him about his degrees, his medical memberships and training, and his specialties. He and Lennon had obviously failed to stipulate those matters. Sometimes lawyers won't agree because they think their doctor or expert has more going as a witness than the opponent's.

Our pathologist's name was Dr. Todd Shanning and he was fortyish, small and wiry. He looked as if he played a lot of tennis. He sat alertly in the witness chair, relaxed and smiling, a good witness. He had pinched features, but was not unattractive. He wore large horn-rimmed glasses and looked intelligent and competent.

"When did you first examine the remains of the fire victim found in the home of Avery Benjamin, Doctor?"

Shanning consulted a thick sheaf of notes. "I was called into the case in April, two and a half years ago."

"And who called you into the case?" Jake asked.

"The Drew County coroner first. Later, two insurance companies holding policies on the life of Avery Benjamin approached me. I examined the remains a total of five times and performed a large number of tests. I spent a total of some eighteen hours examining the remains and performing those various tests."

"You are being paid to testify here in court today by those insurance companies?"

"I'd hope so," Shanning said, smiling.

Several on the jury chuckled and Judge Keeler gave them a stern look, quelling them.

"But your pay or rate of pay is not contingent in any way on what happens in this case?"

"Of course not."

"Tell the jury what you observed."

"The victim of the fire had been quite badly burned. The victim was a white male, well nourished, probably in his mid- to late fifties. The fire had been intense and long-lasting and was undoubtedly fed by accelerants."

Lennon was on his feet, his face angry. "Move to strike the

last part of the doctor's statement. If the fire was fed by accelerants, then the doctor could only have known that by hearsay."

"It may go out," Judge Keeler said. "Do you desire me to admonish the jury concerning the testimony?"

"Not just now," Lennon said. He'd looked over at Jake and seen Jake's half-smile and now was not so positive. *Do not become passionate about arguments the other side may win.*

"Did you find anything in your examination to indicate that the fire in which the victim died had been fed by accelerants?" Jake continued, unperturbed.

"Of course. There was, about the body, the smell of petroleum products. I could smell them during my examination."

Lennon was up again, more hesitant now. "This witness has been qualified as an expert in some areas, but not in those of smell."

Jake smiled some more and warmed to the fight. "Is part of your training as a pathologist based on developing your sense of smell, Doctor?"

"Of course it is. And sight and touch."

"And do you occasionally use the sense of smell in making your medical determinations?" Jake continued.

"Yes. At times. In deaths by poisons, sometimes traces of the poison ingested can be smelled. And in fire deaths sometimes one can smell accelerants, particularly if those accelerants have been placed on the deceased. I could smell them on this occasion. Quite strongly."

"He may testify concerning same, then," Judge Keeler said.

Lennon sat back down and closed a law book in front of him with a snap. Judge Keeler glared down at him and he subsided.

Jake bowed slightly and went back to it.

"Okay, Dr. Shanning. Go ahead."

"In my opinion the victim was dead before the fire. There

was no smoke in what was left of his lungs. There was immense damage to his bones from the fire, and the heat had also, in my opinion, altered the blood, so that any blood-typing became, thereafter, unreliable and useless. About all I had to work with was a lump of burned body material smelling strongly of petroleum products. In my opinion the victim had either had those petroleum products poured upon him or something inside the house had exploded and he'd been sprayed with them."

"Sprayed or poured," Jake mused for the jury.

Lennon was up. "Your honor, I'll object to counsel repeating lines."

"We'll order them stricken," Judge Keeler said, unperturbed.

"How about teeth?" Jake asked.

"The deceased was toothless and there was no plate found."

"Was that consistent with the information you had on the missing Avery Benjamin?"

"Yes. And with millions of others."

Lennon was on his feet. "Move to strike the last sentence of the answer as unresponsive."

"It can go out," the judge said. Again his ruling was emotionless.

"Do you know the percentage number of persons over fifty who wear dentures?"

"Not exactly. It's quite high."

Jake nodded, satisfied. "Did you compare X rays of one Avery Benjamin with the remaining available bones of the person you examined?" Jake asked.

"I did. Once again, the bones had been damaged so much by the heat that no sensible match could be made."

"After all your examinations were made, did you come to a medical opinion as to whether or not the body you examined was that of Avery Benjamin?"

"I did."

"What is that opinion?"

"In my medical opinion the body was not that of Avery Benjamin."

"On what evidence do you base that opinion, Dr. Shanning?"

Shanning shook his head. "I cannot say that the body I saw positively was not that of Avery Benjamin. Extreme, prolonged heat can make identification difficult. My opinion is that the body was not that of Avery Benjamin. I had a copy of Mr. Benjamin's driver's license. I had physical descriptions of him given me by those who knew him and from previous medical examinations which were available to me. Those descriptions indicated Benjamin had a body weight of about two hundred pounds, a height of seventy-three inches. In my opinion the body I saw would have been, in life, substantially smaller than that, perhaps sixty-eight inches, and weighed no more than one hundred fifty pounds in life."

"So can you then state with reasonable medical certainty whether or not the body you examined was that of Avery Benjamin?"

"I can. In my opinion it wasn't Avery Benjamin's body."

The courtroom buzzed a little and Jake waited until it quieted.

"Do you know whose body it was in actuality?"

"No."

Jake went on. I could tell he'd done his homework. He had Dr. Shanning talk about the effect of intense and long-lasting heat on bones and blood. Then they engaged in a spirited discussion concerning the lack of smoke in the lungs and what that meant. What I got was that the corpse had been dead before it was burned.

I watched the jurors. Some of them were interested. Others seemed less so, staring down at the floor, yawning.

Behind the bench Judge Keeler surveyed all. He had a face

that sometimes mirrored his emotions. Now and then he smiled a little as he watched the jury. I wondered what joke he heard in his mind. Now and then he frowned at Jake or Lennon. Frowns appeared more often than smiles.

Lennon whispered to his client. She opened her Bible and began to read studiously. *Shades of Cherry Benjamin. Another born-again.*

A few on the jury watched her. I thought more might have watched her if she'd come into the courtroom looking as she had when I'd entered her web for a few tense moments on Saturday night.

Jake was still going strong when it came time for a midmorning recess. I filed out with a few of the other spectators. Most stayed in their seats, perhaps afraid they'd lose them, but I'd had enough trial for the morning. I figured Jake and Dr. Shanning and cross-examination of the doctor would take the rest of the morning.

On the first floor of the courthouse below I spotted Sam. He was visiting some of the offices there, distributing subpoenas. We carefully and by plan ignored each other. Although some knew who I was, others didn't.

I fell in behind Sam and followed at a distance.

He'd told me, the night before, that he now knew most of the elected officials of Drew County by sight. He was using that knowledge. He entered the commissioner's room. I watched at the door while he interrupted a meeting and served three gentlemen, two in work clothes, the third wearing a suit. They sat around an oval table talking in low tones until Sam appeared.

"You can't do this," one man pointed out to Sam. "It ain't legal."

Sam shrugged amiably and adopted his Uncle Tom brogue. "I just doin' like I told, Mr. Commissioner. Them people I works for makes me do all this kind of bad stuff." He shook his head mournfully. "Never get to go to court, never get to represent no one 'cept po' black folks." He turned away, job performed. At the door he gave me a wink so tiny I wasn't sure of it. Jake and I privately agreed he was the best lawyer we'd seen and his future was limitless. He was immensely bright. We wondered how long we'd be able to keep him happy in Bington.

The two men in work clothes cleared out immediately. I saw one of them walk down the street, perhaps going to Benjamin Construction. The other got into a pickup truck and drove away. The third one, the one in a suit, stood morosely by the window looking out at the Drewville streets.

I approached him. I waved my press card vaguely at him.

"I know that black guy," I said. "He used to play football down at the U. in Bington. Jim Queen, I think. Bington boy. Is he a lawyer or something now? What's he doing up here? What kind of papers did he serve on you?"

The man in the suit was about seventy. He wore a suit that needed pressing and a food-spotted tie with a Rotary emblem centered on it.

"Wants us to go to court to testify on Avery Benjamin's case is all I know," he said. "Name's Sam King, not Jim Queen."

I smiled my thanks for his correction. "I was just up covering that trial. What can you tell me about Avery Benjamin? Is he dead or not?"

He eyed me carefully, but smiled. "I can't tell you or him one single, blessed thing."

"Was Benjamin about to be indicted upstate by the federals when he vanished? Something about a road scam? I heard them lawyers talking."

"I don't know nothing about no road scams," he said coldly. He looked back out the window.

"Plural, eh? Scams? I heard Benjamin was supposed to be paying off a big bunch of people and that a whole new list of witnesses got served on the prosecutor and the judge today,"

I said. I eyed him calculatingly. "What would your name be, mister?"

"Excuse me," he said, pushing past me. "I got to be someplace and I'm already late."

"I'll be in court tomorrow," I said. "I'll get your name then and use it."

He stopped and straightened. For a moment I was sure he was going to turn back to me, but then he went on. From the window I watched him. He went down the street in the direction of Benjamin Construction also. Maybe it was headquarters.

A young girl at a desk on the far side of the big commissioner's room said, "You aren't supposed to be in here, mister. I wouldn't care that much, but it's time for my coffee break."

I smiled at her. "Why's everyone in this little town so jumpy?" I asked. "Ask a question and everyone runs out as quick and quiet as they can. And there's all these fires."

She shook her head, not knowing or not saying.

"And why did two of those commissioners go from here up to Benjamin Construction?"

She shrugged and got up. "Office is closed," she announced coldly. "Now you get on out or I'll call our sheriff."

That seemed sufficient reason to smile and leave.

CHAPTER EIGHT

Steinmetz's Axiom: "The wise lawyer won't finally decide what a witness will testify to until he hears it from the witness stand."

That afternoon I got my second look at Cherry Benjamin, Avery's first wife, when Jake called her to testify.

I'd not gotten as good a seat as I'd had in the morning, but I did have a seat about halfway back. She came into the courtroom and was sworn and seated. I craned between the spectators in front of me and examined her again.

She'd cleaned up from when I'd seen her briefly in her front yard with a rake. She was out of the bulky, ugly clothes. I figured her weight at close to two hundred and she was maybe six feet tall. She was cunningly dressed to hide the weight and she looked all right, straight and tall and still strong. Her iron-gray hair was combed and set, and only her eyes, with large dark marks in the skin under them, looked bad. Her face was more patrician than pretty, a forceful face with large, slightly hooked nose and carved lips. I knew she was in her early sixties and that she'd divorced Avery Benjamin (or he'd divorced her?) some five years back.

If she was still some kind of secret drinker, which Jake seemed to think when I'd discussed her with him, there were no overt signs of it now except for the dark marks under her eyes.

She walked to the witness stand and took her seat there. Her step was as silent and careful as an Indian's.

Jake led her through identification testimony. On the other side of the courtroom, Damon Lennon watched and listened warily.

"You are the former wife of the alleged deceased?"

"Yes," she answered crisply, smiling at him.

"And the mother of two of the claimants or plaintiffs in this trial?"

"I am. My two sons. Eric and Fritz."

"How long were you and Avery Benjamin married?"

"More than thirty years."

"When you were married to Mr. Benjamin, did he like to play jokes on people?"

"Yes. He did that all the time. He was a great and inventive joker, Mr. Bornstein."

That was something I'd not known of, so I leaned forward to hear better.

"What kind of jokes was he fondest of?"

Damon Lennon was on his feet. "I'm going to object. Jokes that he pulled five years or more ago wouldn't have anything to do with his personality at the time of his death."

"Alleged death," Jake said, correcting Lennon.

"Objection sustained."

Jake shrugged and ventured further. "Do you know your former husband's new wife?"

"Of course. This is a small town," Cherry said coolly. She nodded over at Hilda Benjamin and smiled widely at something, perhaps the Bible in front of Hilda. "I know her. She knows me. We don't much like each other, but that's normal, I suppose. She got Avery and I got a good settlement. Knowing Avery, maybe I got the best deal."

I saw Hilda's hands tighten, but her face didn't change.

"Did you attend your former husband's funeral?" Jake continued.

"Yes. I went. Along with half the town. Recreational therapy." She smiled a little. "Of course I feel different about it now and I pray for him some."

"After the fire at his home, did you ever see Avery Benjamin again?"

She stared at Jake. An alarm bell rang loudly inside my brain.

She shook her head. "No. He's dead. Sometimes, maybe because I was drinking heavy or something, I'd think I'd seen him or that he'd called me. I told that to those insurance people who were slipping and sneaking around and are still slipping and sneaking around here, meddling in Drewville. Now I'm sober and have been for a good little while. I know seeing him after he died in his home was just a dream." She smiled. "A figment of my imagination." She nodded and her voice was sure. "Avery's dead."

Jake, in perfect control, went to his counsel table and conferred with Sam. The damage was done. I silently prayed they'd let it stop right where it was and not go after her and hurt themselves further. The judge had said he'd not let in prior statements and I'd seen no depositions in the file. Raymond Lucas had not taken any, perhaps not thinking he'd need them, and we'd gotten in the case too late to do them.

Jake stood up. "No more questions," he said, perhaps reading my mind.

Damon Lennon stood up. I thought he was as surprised as Jake had been, but substantially more pleased. He looked the big, gray lady over, as if unsure about her. To ask or not to ask. That was the problem.

"No questions," he said finally. I approved.

She was excused. She got up and walked stolidly out of the courtroom. From the rear corner of the courtroom I saw the sheriff. For the first time he was smiling as he eyed me. I ignored the smile. I got up, left the courtroom, and followed behind Cherry Benjamin at a distance. I looked over my shoulder and saw that the sheriff was following me.

Cherry Benjamin went down the steps. Outside, she nodded at one or two people she knew. I sat down on a cold,
vacant bench in the courthouse yard and watched her. She
pulled her coat tight around her and walked directly to the
office-store of the Benjamin Construction Company. She entered the door there.

I waited. Behind me, at the courthouse door, I could see
Sheriff House watching me through the glass. Maybe he
thought I'd go after Cherry Benjamin and try to shake the
truth out of her. But all I wanted to do was observe.

When I was about to give up and go back into the warm
courthouse, I saw Cherry Benjamin come out. One of her
strong sons was with her. They drove away in a ten-year-old
Ford truck. They seemed pretty cheery and chummy.

I walked around the block a couple of times. Each time I
passed the courthouse main door, I nodded cheerily up at
Sheriff House. The third time around he was gone, either
having given up or moved to some other unseen vantage
point to watch me. I then walked up a block and over several
blocks in case he was still watching. I entered the office-store
of the Benjamins from the back way. No one seemed to be
following. Behind a rail the remaining brother, the one with
the Orphan Annie eyes, sat at an old adding machine working the handle. He looked up and saw me.

"Be with you in a moment," he said. He looked strong and
efficient. His eyes were a peculiar hazel that was almost yellow. I didn't like to watch them or him.

Along a far wall I found a thin extension ladder made of
aluminum, weighing maybe fifteen pounds. I discovered I
could hoist, carry, and maneuver it easily. It appeared to be
the only one in stock. In another aisle I found a few spades. I
tested their edges with my finger and picked out a sharp one.
By that time Cherry's son was beside me.

"Doing some work?" he asked, yellow eyes interested. I
thought, but wasn't positive, that he knew me.

"Going to do some soon," I said, smiling at him. "Are you Eric or Fritz?"

"Fritz," he answered shortly. "Eric's eyes is blue. Lots of people think we're twins, but we ain't. I'm two years older than him. Some say he's the nice one. I never argue about that." He totaled the two purchases, added tax, and I paid him in cash.

"Looks like a strong ladder," I said.

"We've had no complaints on them. Wood's heavier and stronger. Got a couple of them, if you'd prefer. Happy to take your money. We need it here in Drewville. All contributions gratefully accepted."

"This one will do fine for the job I have in mind," I said.

He eyed me carefully and again I thought he knew who I was. Maybe I'd been known from the time I set foot in Drewville. In a town the size of Drewville it was possible, and I now wondered if someone had been watching me from the first moment I'd entered the small town.

I escaped his eyes by carrying the purchases away with me. I walked with them through the cold streets a mile or so to the edge of Drewville. There I unlocked the Plymouth. The ladder would only fit in it if I shoved it in over the front seat, resting one end in the back left and the other crosswise against the inner, right-hand windshield. That left me barely enough room to drive.

I put the spade on the back floor.

I started the car and looked at the digital clock, which spelled out the time in lighted numbers. Not quite two o'clock on a cold afternoon. Jake and Sam would be doing battle for the rest of the afternoon with routine stuff. They could tell me about it tonight.

It still felt like snow coming to me.

If snow was coming, I wanted to look at the place where Raymond Lucas, the insurance companies' lawyer until he'd died, had gone over Cemetery Hill. I drove up the hill slowly.

There was no other way to drive it. A few cars passed me, going down, but no one was behind me. Corporal Cadwell, of the state police, had said I could find the spot because of a skinned tree.

Even driving slow I missed the tree when I drove past it and only found it when I turned around and came back toward town.

The skinned spot on the tree had darkened from time and the weather, but I saw it plainly enough. There was a pull-off area nearby, so I parked and got out and walked back to the tree.

I wondered if Lucas had tried to hit the tree. It sat on downgrade. A few steps beyond the tree, the land fell sharply away. Hit the tree right and maybe it'd stop you and you'd live through it.

I walked farther. I could see a couple of places where there'd been mudslides and I could see what I thought was the track that the Lucas car had traversed. A straight fall, the car turning over, then end-for-end. No chance for Lucas. Quick death for a drunken lawyer, or so the world thought.

I walked back to the road and sat in my car. Someone could have done it. Someone could have overpowered Lucas and put him, unconscious, in his car, planted the whiskey, then sent him against the tree and over the edge. But why the tree first? Why not just straight over?

And it could also have been an accident. A long time ago now. Too long for the view here to tell me anything.

Something passed so quickly through my brain that I almost missed it. Something I'd heard. I thought hard, but no light came.

Something.

I drove carefully back down the hill and on to Burger King. There were some other fast-food restaurants nearby, but I ignored them. I got my Whopper with cheese, no onions, plus a cup of coffee. I waited. From a machine near the door I bought a copy of the Drew County *Enquirer-Telephone* and read it for something to do. It was full of homey columns about who'd visited whom and who was in and out of the hospital. The front-page headline had to do with a new county agent in the courthouse. The pages were full of political advertisements, a long column of Washington news from the area congressman, and recipes for goodies. Just the thing to read for a scheming lawyer come to Drewville to do a poor woman out of her insurance money.

About three o'clock, when I was on coffee two and the last page of the paper, the daily youth invasion began. For a time I was afraid that the boy I wanted to see wouldn't appear, but he did about fifteen minutes later. He saw me and came over, grinning, ignoring for the moment a couple of nubile girls who were ogling him.

"There's Sheriff Brick's best buddy," he said.

"That's me. Don Robak, punching bag."

"You did good for an old guy," he said.

"Want a couple more jobs, Ted?" I asked, ignoring the unmeant insult.

He nodded. "Sure. As long as I don't have to carry a gun."

"Any repercussions on the last one?"

"Not yet, Mr. Robak. But he'll try to get us and try to get you." He nodded. "Count on it. Most of us here will be eighteen and voters next time he runs. That's the day we'll get good and even. He couldn't get five votes out of my bunch. And we're going to work to make sure people know about him. Come election day, there'll be an army of us out there at the polls."

"That's good. It's the way to do it."

"What is it you want?"

"I need someone to look around down across the river from where they were building the nuke plant. Avery Benjamin was supposed to have a hunting and fishing place down there. I'll be looking myself, maybe tomorrow, but I don't

know what I'm looking for. If you've got friends of yours who
fish or boat much, maybe they will. I'll take a chance."

"How many guys you want?"

"Half a dozen, maybe. No one who'll get lost. Hunter and
fisherman types. And I want them to spread the word about
what they're doing around the town so it gets back to the
sheriff. If anyone finds anything, call me tonight at this number—collect. If you find anything not worth the call, then tie
a handkerchief to a limb by it or something. Maybe I'll see it."

"We'll try, but I never heard of a cabin down there. Avery
Benjamin—I heard he was part Indian. If he wanted to hide
something, it'd stay hid." He looked me over curiously. "You
said jobs. What's the other one?"

"I want someone to tell me if Cherry Benjamin is hung up
with some church called the Redeemer Church."

"I can tell you that. A couple of the kids in high school go
there. She's one of the high dogs in it."

"Check it out anyway. I'll pay ten bucks an hour."

"You got it." He started to move away and then returned.
I waited.

He shrugged. "How much for checking the woods?"

We bargained for a while.

I waited some more while he spread the word and gath-
ered together some of his followers.

They left exuberantly to begin. Two carloads of boys. Plus a
single watcher for the church.

When they were gone I drove the twenty miles or so to our
new motel and waited there for Jake and Sam to return from
the courtroom wars. I parked the car at the far end of the
buildings, away from where they'd have to pass. No need for
them to see my new purchases. They might upset Jake.

After a joyless motel supper the three of us went to the
room.

"I guess I should have known she'd probably do that," Jake

said. "You warned me," he said to me. "After all, it's her sons who stand to gain. I figured if we needed to depose her, then Lucas would have done it before he went over the side of the hill road."

"They call it Cemetery Hill, I think."

"Good name for it. There wasn't any time left when we got into it. Discovery time had run. The insurance-company boys are real angry about Cherry, but they got pretty obstinate when I mentioned compromise. They like our chances better than they did. Looks like this one goes to the jury." He looked at me. "You said she tried to call you. Why do you think she did that, Don?"

"I don't know. She told me she was into a religion. Maybe she was going to tell me she was changing her story. But when she got off the stand, she went directly to the store her boys run."

He nodded. "She set us up."

"Possibly. Maybe not. String out your political witnesses tomorrow. Make them last all day if you can."

"Why?"

"I hired some kids to look for Avery Benjamin's fishing and hunting shack. I posted a small reward. I trust your insurance company will pay it. I've also got a kid watching the church Cherry Benjamin is supposed to go to. I'm paying ten bucks an hour for that."

"They'll pay it gladly, but you're crazy," he said. "No kids are going to find Avery Benjamin. He's long gone by now. He won't show up again until the insurance is paid, if ever. His shack won't do us any good. And Cherry's just another crackpot."

"Maybe," I said. "Something in a shack might show us he was alive and well after the critical date. String out your witnesses. And I'd like to see if Cherry's sincere. One kid already told me she was, but I'm double-checking."

"With arguments enough, I can string things out," he said.

He gave me an oblique look. "You going to tell your witnesses to come in Wednesday?"

"I guess. Unless we get a break tomorrow." I looked at my watch. "I'm going to go back to Drewville tonight. I want to do a few things. If you get a collect call, accept it and take the information."

He shrugged, interested, but not much. "This case has you as crazy as it's got me and Sam."

"When I left Drewville this afternoon, the boys I hired were already starting to look." I spread my hands. "Who knows?"

"What's this about a fishing shack?" Sam asked. "Why would Avery Benjamin be hanging around a fishing shack?"

"I heard a story he used to have one that he used for hunting and fishing down someplace near the nuclear plant on one of the branches of the Blue. That's very near where a couple of our witnesses saw him. Maybe if I can find the shack, I can find evidence of his being there after the date he was supposed to have died. I've got a theory. I think he not only wants to take the insurance companies, I think he also wants to rub their noses in it."

Jake shook his head. "I still say that even if he once had one, he'd be smart enough not to be hanging around the county with the trial going on and smart enough not to leave you any evidence of any kind."

"Our witnesses say he either wasn't that smart or he was that arrogant before. Maybe we'll get lucky."

Jake and Sam looked at each other and Sam shook his head warningly. "Good luck, then."

"Touched in the head you are," Jake said to me, smiling. "Crazy as a one-armed fighter pilot. Always trying to make things into a plot."

I drove back to Drewville, staying within the speed limit, watching for official-looking vehicles. I saw none.

First off, I drove past Cherry Benjamin's place, but it was

dark. She was either an early-to-bed lady or she was out someplace, probably at the church.

I then drove past Hilda Benjamin's house at slow speed. The lights were off there also, and for Hilda that meant a ninety-percent chance she was out partying. I wanted her inside her home. I didn't want to be about my job and have her suddenly appear with her bosom pal the sheriff.

I parked down the street and settled back in my seat. With the ladder in the car it was hard to nap because my head kept snapping over against it and the aluminum was cold and hard. I managed to sleep now and then. I was tired. The car was icy and the coldness woke me up after each short nap.

About midnight the sheriff's car eased past mine without slowing and the gate to Hilda Benjamin's place opened. I rolled my window down despite the cold and listened and watched.

Sheriff House parked his car on the far edge of the driveway, where I'd parked my car once. He got out and I saw him open the other door. A female voice called him a foul name, but the tone wasn't angry, only playful. *Now for a few games and a bit of late-night frivolity.*

They supported each other up the steps. A light went on downstairs, then upstairs, then, after a while, there was darkness.

I forced myself to wait another full hour. I got the ladder and the spade out of the car and took them down the alley to the neighboring garage I'd spotted before. I extended the ladder to its farthest point, hooked it, and tied it with cord, and scrambled up it onto the garage roof, carrying the spade. Once there, I stopped everything and crouched silently, listening.

Nothing. They could be waiting for me, but I thought they'd been out celebrating Cherry's testimony. An unexpected bonus maybe. They'd acted like they'd had more than a few drinks when they'd gotten out of the car. They should be out for a good long while.

A tiny snowflake fell, then another, then nothing. The wind made goose bumps rise along my back.

Life was a gamble. I dropped the spade into Hilda's yard, pulled the ladder up and put it from garage top into Hilda's yard. I went silently down after my spade. I found some likely spots and made holes, front yard and back. The ground was hard on top, but the sharp spade made the work easy and fast.

When I had about twenty holes dug, all without result, I gave it up for the night. I took the spade and went back up the ladder. I got the ladder unhooked and put it and the spade back into Jo's car and drove back to the twenty-mile motel.

With some wet paper towels from the washroom in the motel lobby I washed the spade down well. I also scoured the feet of the ladder. I went back inside once and got more towels, wet them and soaped them and repeated the task. When I was done, the feet of the ladder, the places it had touched the roof, and the spade were spotless. Maybe a lab exam could find something that could be traced to Hilda's area on the spade and ladder, but nothing less than that kind of examination would do it. And I doubted the land near Hilda's house was that different from its neighbors.

I placed the ladder at its minimum length and put it under my bed. The ladder stuck out a little bit, so I turned it some so that it was harder to see. I put the spade on top of it. I wondered what the maid would think.

I left a call for six in the morning and had about four hours of good, dreamless sleep.

In the morning, when the call came, I caught the phone quickly and rolled out of bed, ready for the new day. Jake eyed me from his door.

"What time is it?"

"Six."

"My alarm's set for seven. You got one call last night. A kid said Cherry spent all evening at some church. He said you owed him forty bucks."

I nodded. "I'll see you sometime later today."

He shook his head, his eyes sleepy. "Where are you going?" He looked into my room. "And what's that ladder doing under your bed?"

I looked. The ladder and spade were plainly visible where I'd pulled away the blanket and sheet when I'd rolled out of bed.

"I picked those up at Benjamin's yesterday. I need them both at home. Good ladder, good spade."

He eyed me distrustfully. "Where are you going now?"

"Out on the river." I smiled. "If I don't get back, you have those numbers to call for tomorrow's witnesses. Be calm and nice when you call. Try to sound casual and uncaring."

He nodded. "Just exactly what is it you're up to?"

"I'm not sure yet. I'll tell you if anything comes of it."

CHAPTER NINE

"Direct contempt of court is contemptuous behavior committed in the presence of the court."

For thirty dollars I rented a boat with a small outboard motor from a taciturn and arthritic old man who seemed surprised to have me knock at his door in the dim light of such a dismal morning.

"You're way out of season, boy," he grumbled. But he limped outside with me and we went first to his boat shed and then to his dock. He shivered in the cold and said, "You're going to freeze the whole ass end of you off out there on the river."

I nodded somberly. The weather was cold and there was a gusting wind. Now and then there'd be a brief shower of something halfway between rain and sleet. I'd not liked that driving to Drewville, but the asphalt road, perhaps because the ground was still warm underneath, had resisted the freezing rain and stayed wet and safe. Now it had grown perceptibly colder. Here and there the ice and snow were sticking in tiny spots.

The Blue River was full of waves, some with whitecaps. The old man eyed my thin, lined raincoat with suspicion and made me show him my driver's license again before I was allowed to launch and embark in the shabby motorboat he'd made me wheel from his boat shed while he drank black coffee from a tin cup. He didn't offer me any.

"There's a life jacket under the boat seat. Wear it," he

advised. "There's places on this river where, if you fall in, you'll drown quick without a life jacket." He shook his head once more. "It's going to get a lot colder. I can feel it in my poor old bones. The life jacket might help with the cold, too. If I was you, I wouldn't go too far, boy."

"How about gasoline?" I asked, putting on the life jacket.

"Plenty of gas in the tank to keep your little fifteen horse on the back there going all day and all night. You won't run out of gas. And that's a good, steady motor." He gave me a thin, jackknife smile. "You'll freeze inside your itty-bitty raincoat a long time before you're out of gas."

"Thanks for the advice," I said. I got the boat running after a few yanks. He stood on his dock and watched my awkwardness, shaking his head now and then, his hand clutched tight around the money I'd given him. I wondered if he thought I was a drowner, renting his boat to commit suicide and commit it in such a fashion that it could be ruled an accident. It happened. At least it did at Bington, where I practiced law when I was in my right senses.

Fifty yards down the whitecapped river I turned to wave at him, but he'd already gone back inside, perhaps to warm his coffee. Whatever and whoever I was, he had his thirty dollars in cash and I was on my own.

It was frigid. So, very soon, was I. The temperature had to be in the mid-thirties, but with the wind coming at me, it seemed more like the low teens. The life jacket was bulky and it did help a little, but it only covered a small part of my body and it flapped and gapped in the wind. I had no gloves and my hands were soon like two blocks of ice. Now and then, to warm one, I'd put it inside my coat, but until I caught on to how to operate the little boat I needed both hands most of the time. The boat bucked its way through the waves.

I found the best way to do it was to stay close to shore. The wind seemed less a factor there. I headed the boat downstream toward the nuclear plant. I fought the waves, fearful

I'd turn over, but the boat rode well and high in the water and was probably safer than I believed it to be.

I was sleepy, but the cold kept me awake.

It took about an hour to get to the abandoned nuclear plant. All the time I kept up a watch along the far shore, looking for something, anything. There were a few houses, but most of them were high up on the hills that rose in the distance. The ground along the Blue until the rise near the plant was flood plain and only the foolish built cabins there. Besides, what I sought wasn't going to show up easily.

A few snowflakes dotted the ground and slowly melted. The mist in the air was icy. I looked up at the sky and thought there was more coming. It seemed to me it was growing colder.

When I saw the containment towers I guided the boat to the far side of the river, the side where witnesses claimed to have seen Avery Benjamin. I throttled down the motor. The boys I'd hired yesterday would have searched along here. Perhaps, even though they'd not found enough to mention by telephone, they'd found enough to leave a handkerchief tied somewhere. Maybe they'd only come, made a cursory search, and repaired to the Burger King. At least I knew Cherry Benjamin was in church.

It was hard to stay in the channel, difficult to tell what was main channel and what was not. Dozens of small streams flowed into the Blue, and the river itself, wider here than in Drewville, made its own myriad channels and disguised them as creeks. Some were covered with spreading trees, but now the leaves were gone and I could see up them. I explored them, but there was nothing to find, at least from my vantage point as I sat hunched deep in the boat, freezing in the cold. I wished I'd asked Mark Koontz just exactly where he'd seen Avery Benjamin, I wished my kid searchers had found something and left me a handkerchief, but it was too late to do more than wish now.

I kept exploring side streams and checking the bank along the channels, trying to look for physical things I could recognize again—rocks, big trees, odd shapes to openings into or out of the river. I looked for anything that meant human use —hatchet marks, wear where a boat had been tied, holes in trees, cloth scraps, anything. I saw nothing, particularly nothing that looked like a fishing or hunting shack. I began to believe that the kids I'd hired had given up quickly and gone back to Drewville, and not that they'd just found nothing.

After an hour of searching I was beyond sight of the nuclear plant so I turned back, moving more slowly against the current, but not so cold now with the wind at my back. I'd seen a total of zero. I longed to give it up.

My watch told me it was nearing nine in the morning. Jake and Sam would soon be doing battle in Drewville's courtroom. It was very cold and I thought about just giving it up. I'd gotten them their witnesses, given them a chance. I wondered why I was out here in this cold boat chasing fantasies. Halfway between forty to fifty years old and still chasing will-o'-the-wisps.

On the nuclear plant side, away from where I was, I saw two fishermen casting their lines into the swift, cold water. They were dressed for the weather, but it was still a crazy day to fish. I waved at them. They waved back in the fashion that men will when they see each other committing silly acts like fishing and boating in bad weather.

One of the fishermen looked familiar, so I curiously guided the boat their way, thinking it might be Mark Koontz or one of his friends. If so, I might get directions to where they'd seen the person they thought was Avery Benjamin.

The two men stood on a high rock that jutted out into the river. They cast their lines into the almost still water that the big rock created and protected from the current.

One of the fishermen was Steinmetz. There was shock in the recognition, but then, thinking on it, I smiled. He was not a man to leave you by yourself at a difficult time. So, he was here. He'd helped me in the past—why not Jake and Sam?

"Who's taking care of the office?" I yelled up to him.

He shrugged and grinned. I got a good look at his companion, but didn't know him. I pulled the boat into shore above them and beached it high up after shutting off the motor.

I scrambled through the rocks and confronted the pair.

"Came to watch part of the trial," Steinmetz said, smiling at me. "It sounded interesting. Brought a friend along with me to watch also." He turned to his friend, a man about my age, trim, and with agate-hard eyes. "Jess, this is Don Robak, who keeps things interesting for an old man in his dotage."

Jess smiled and shook my hand. His own hand was calloused and strong. He said nothing. I was curious about him, but restrained it. If I needed to know more I thought Steinmetz would tell me.

"Jess Yanack," he murmured.

The name meant nothing to me. And then it did, vaguely. Something I'd read?

"Lawyer?" I asked politely.

"Was one. I'm a judge now."

"We parked the car up the way off a side road," Steinmetz explained. "We thought we'd get a little fishing in before watching the trial. Jake called last night and said it might be interesting for me to be here today."

"Could be. He didn't say anything about calling you to me."

"He complains you don't tell him much either. He was mighty down last night. He thinks that Judge Keeler is looking for a chance to do something to him. Jake doesn't like the idea of being punished because you gave them a bright idea."

"That's Jake," I said. "He worries a lot." I looked at my watch. "It's after nine. You'll have to watch from the hall."

"I'd imagine," Steinmetz said, not upset about it, "I wouldn't want Amos to see me anyway. Might bother him, affect his official-type decisions. Have you met Judge Keeler yet?"

"Not formally. I've been in and out of the courtroom some. I think he knows who I am. In fact, I'd bet on it. A lot of Drewville citizens seem to know a lot about me. Keeler's an abrupt man."

"That's Amos all right," Steinmetz said. "What are you doing out on the river in this kind of weather?"

"Looking around. A couple of our witnesses claim to have seen Avery Benjamin near here a little while back. And I heard a story about a cabin. I was looking for it or whatever else I could find."

"We've not seen anyone but you," Steinmetz said. "Want to come watch the trial with us for a while?"

"There's the boat," I said, wanting to go watch, but not knowing how.

"Leave it here. Unhook the gas tank and put it in the back of the car. No one will bother the boat here on a day like this. Only fools and lawyers, and those two words may be synonymous, go boating or fishing in this kind of weather."

I was cold and frustrated and hungry. "Will you bring me back this afternoon? I want to walk the shore over on the other side, but not until I get some heavier clothes. It's cold."

"Sure. Steinmetz's sterling taxi service." He nodded at Jess. "We won't catch anything this morning. Too cold, too rough. Sorry about that, Jess."

Yanack smiled and nodded and I wondered again about him. But people were always stopping by to see Steinmetz. He had a million friends.

They waited while I unscrewed the gas-tank hose and took the gas tank. I pulled the boat up even higher on the shore and covered it with some branches. I stored the gas tank in the trunk of Steinmetz's car.

I had them drop me at Babe's and I went in and had some eggs and bacon and three cups of hot black coffee. My waitress served me silently.

"I was out on the river this morning," I said to her in a low voice. "Looking for that cabin you spoke of."

She nodded and looked apprehensively toward the kitchen.

"I didn't find anything," I finished.

"I don't know where it is," she said. "And I've heard you're really a lawyer and not a reporter like you said. Are you?"

"I'm both."

"A lot of people been talking about you."

"Saying what, Milly?"

"Mean, nasty things. Them Benjamin boys come in here. I heard them talking. Was I you, I'd watch out for them. The one of them with the funny eyes, he's not quite right in the head. I think he got dropped some when he was a baby." She smiled.

"When was this that they were in talking about me?"

"The afternoon of the first day you was in here. Then they were in again early this morning and I heard your name. Their momma was with them. First time I've seen the three of them together for a time."

"You mean Cherry?"

"Yes. Hilda would still be in bed this time of day."

She'd wake up sooner or later and see my depredations. I wondered what would happen when she did.

The courtroom was overflowing again and so I stood at the back entrance. The coffee and breakfast had warmed me some. Steinmetz stood slightly away from the door, his head bent, out of line of sight for Judge Keeler. But Jess Yanack had shouldered his way right up to the door and watched intently from there.

I looked around inside the courtroom. Somehow the word

had spread that things were about to happen. I saw reporters from some of the nearby city newspapers in attendance, making notes, watching. The politicians in Drew County were probably mighty upset. And maybe nervous.

Inside, Jake and Sam were bravely making offers to prove. The jury was absent for now, probably closeted in their jury room enjoying coffee and rolls. The sheriff was on the stand. He saw me at the courtroom door and recognized me as the author of his woes. He glared out at me and Judge Keeler, catching his glance, added his own glare. I smiled gently at them.

"Now, Sheriff House, having stated your name and told us about the county office you hold, can you tell us about any criminal difficulties that Avery Benjamin was having at the time he disappeared or died?"

Lennon was on his feet. His demeanor was one of tiredness, almost boredom, of a man who was putting up with the slings and arrows of an uncertain world. "Objection. Same reason as before."

"Sustained," Judge Keeler said. His face was red and angry, his voice irritated. I was glad I wasn't in one of the counsel chairs. Lawyers know it's a judge's world. They merely try to live in it, to survive, sometimes to prosper.

"Offer to prove that if the witness had been allowed to answer, he'd have testified that Avery Benjamin was a target in a federal grand jury investigation concerning his road-building business and certain irregularities therein," Jake said.

"That has nothing to do with this trial," Keeler said. "I've already advised you of that."

"May I go on?" Jake asked politely.

Keeler hesitated. "Proceed, Mr. Bornstein," Judge Keeler said, making Jake's name sound like an epithet.

Jake stiffened a little, but then he turned back to the sheriff. "How many other area citizens were also targets in that investigation, Sheriff House?"

"Objection. Same reasons."

"Sustained."

"Offer to prove that if the witness had been allowed to answer, he would have stated that there were numerous other area officials involved in the investigation as targets: county councilmen, commissioners, road superintendents, and perhaps the sheriff himself." Jake nodded. "I'll read their names into the record or, if the court will, he can read them himself from the new witness list we offered."

"Now wait a minute," Sheriff House said. "I wasn't targeted. All they'd done was talk to me, offer me immunity. They wanted to know who'd given me campaign money. That's all."

Judge Keeler held up a hand. "You needn't have answered, Sheriff." He looked out at Jake. "And the court will order your answer stricken." He nodded at Jake. "The way you're putting it, Mr. Bornstein, just about everyone in Drew County is some kind of crook or thief."

Jake shook his head. "For the record, that's the court's statement and not mine, your honor."

Keeler smiled terribly. "That little remark's going to cost you a night in the Drew County cooler, Mr. Bornstein. That's direct contempt." He gave his court reporter a little wave of the hand and I saw her flick a switch on her recording equipment. We were off the record.

"I apologize to the court if the court misunderstood my reply," Jake said. "I merely meant that you said that in open court and I did not. It was said so that the official transcript would reflect that it was the court making the remark. There are, of course, many honest people in Drew County."

"Too late now," Judge Keeler said. "The court's found you in contempt and you're going to do a day in jail."

Sam rose at the counsel table. "He's already told you he meant nothing, Judge Keeler."

Keeler considered him. "You can join him, *Mister* King. You've already been told it's one lawyer at a time in this courtroom. This court gave you no leave to speak." He looked around his courtroom, smiling a little now, very sure of himself and his power. "Anyone else here to complain?" His eyes sought and found me at his door. "How about you, Mr. Robak? I've heard it said that you're the ringleader of this crew of character assassins."

"How about me?" Jess Yanack asked loudly from beside me. "I'll ask you to have your court reporter turn her recorder back on, Judge Keeler. And I'll also ask that the remarks made since she turned it off become a part of the record. I'd hate to be in your shoes if you send a transcript north without them."

"And just who the hell would you be, sir?"

"If you'll send your bailiff back I'll present my card. Read it." Yanack's voice was cold as the snow that fell outside.

Behind me I heard Steinmetz whisper. "Get out of my way, Don. I want him to see me here while they're taking the card up. I want the arrogant bastard to know who set him up."

I stepped aside and pushed back and Steinmetz moved into my place beside Jess Yanack. He grinned wolfishly up at Keeler.

"Who the hell is Jess?" I whispered into Steinmetz's ear. He ignored me.

A bailiff came and took the card Jess proffered. He delivered it to Keeler and Keeler examined it. I saw his color change from red to white. He looked down at the bench top for a long moment, pondering.

"The court will recess for a few moments. Leave the jury as they are in the jury room, Mr. Bailiff. Get them some more coffee if they want it. Let's keep them out of this for now."

Judge Keeler nodded out to Steinmetz and Jess. "Gentlemen, let's retire to my chambers along with Mr. Bornstein, Mr. King, and Mr. Lennon."

On the stand the sheriff watched all with amazement in his eyes. He whispered something furiously to the judge and got a swift hand motion cutting him off in midsentence.

"Step down, Sheriff House. Wait in the hall until we're done."

Not having been invited to the conference, I waited in the hall also. I endured Sheriff House's stare and his muttered words when I walked past him.

A reporter I vaguely knew approached me.

"What's going on, Don?"

I shook my head. "I swear I don't know. I don't really know the guy who sent his card to the judge. His name's Jess Yanack. He said he was a judge when I asked. He looked familiar or the name sounded familiar, but I don't know him. I guess Steinmetz does."

The reporter smiled. "I know him. He served as the deputy supreme court administrator for a short time earlier this year. The governor named him to the appellate court last week. Used to be a mean prosecutor up north. He's also on the Disciplinary Board. I thought he looked familiar when he first started talking." He grinned. "Jess Yanack. Out doing missionary work among the savages."

"How'd you find out something was going on here in Drewville?"

"Had a call. Anonymous. Some of the other papers had calls also. Very interesting so far. I haven't had so much fun since I covered the Carteret murder case."

I nodded and waited. So did the reporter. After a long while Jake came out of the judge's chambers. His eyes sought and found me. He motioned to me.

When I got to him he leaned close. "Would you settle for a

mistrial?" he asked. "Keeler will disqualify himself and we'll get ourselves a brand-new judge and another trial."

"Up to you. It's your case." I could see problems both ways.

He shook his head, unable to decide. "I don't know what to do. We'd surely be better off in some ways in six months, but in others we might be worse. I hate not finishing it. I think the jury senses that there's something up. We bring in your witnesses it's going to be devastating for the other side."

"How about your night in jail?"

"No jail. Judge Keeler has agreed it was all a misunderstanding and that we meant no disrespect for the court. His face looked like sour apples when he was saying it, but that's the way it is. And we had the court reporter in so it's on the record."

"Pity," I said, grinning. "He wanted us all, you know. Me, you, and Sam."

"That was plain."

"Do you have to decide on a mistrial now?"

"No. In fact, we can't. The judge wants to break and start again in the morning. I think all of this shook him up. He's a man running for reelection and here comes someone out of the courts upstate looking hard at him and talking about possible disciplinary proceedings. Besides, there are heavy snow warnings and he wants to get the jury out of here before the snow comes."

I thought about it. Time was time, and it should work in our favor. "Let's talk some more and decide in the morning."

He looked me over. "I wish you'd tell me exactly what have you got going, Don?"

"A little mischief already committed. If we can decide tomorrow and I can have the time, I'd like to have it. See what happens when the pressure is on the other side and their feet are close by the fire."

He eyed me narrowly and then suddenly smiled. "Well,

you helped some and so I'll say we're thinking on it, but haven't yet decided. All right?"

"All right. And tell Steinmetz I need the gas tank for my boat." I looked down the hall and out a far window. It was snowing pretty good out there now.

CHAPTER TEN

Steinmetz's Advice: "The best place for a lawyer to play hide and seek is in a courtroom, not out in the open country."

Along the Blue River the snow was beginning to stick to the ground in patches. The air had grown colder, but I was warmer now.

I'd gone into one of Drewville's dime-and-dollar stores and bought myself a cheap cotton sweater and a pair of heavy gloves and some rubber pullovers for my shoes. I'd then talked Steinmetz into delivering me back to the side road near the abandoned nuclear plant where the boat was beached.

He'd shook his head when he let me out of the car. "There's nothing for you out there but bad weather, Don. And it's going to get real bad." He looked up at the dark sky with an experienced eye. "Get the boat and run it back to where you rented it. Then we'll meet at the motel and have a drink to celebrate. I guess you could say that we've won. The insurance companies are full of joy and the Jake-and-Sam team are a success no matter what happens now."

I'd almost said yes. But the fact that a someone who at least looked like Avery Benjamin had been seen again and again in this area and I'd not finished looking it over made me shake my head.

"I'll take a quick trip over and a walk up the far bank. Then I'll run the boat back, and be with you guys before long. When I get there, someone can retell me exactly what happened in Judge Keeler's office. That must have been an interesting time."

Steinmetz grunted noncommittally and disapprovingly watched me vanish into the snow, carrying the gasoline tank for the boat.

The snowflakes were large and almost as wet as rain. They stuck to my coat and pants and to my hair, making me into a walking snowman. I let the boat slide through their white veil and found the far shore. I cruised along with the motor throttled down as low as it would go. Now and then, in a place or two, it seemed to me I could smell wood smoke. When I was out of range of the smell I tested the wind with a wet finger and tried to determine what direction the smoke was coming from. I'd quit cigarettes years before and now I smelled everything. The smoke odor was very faint, but it was there. Maybe it was from someone burning leaves, but I thought not in this weather, with the heavy, wet snow coming down.

I turned back and found a side stream that I'd not noticed before. I maneuvered the boat up it. The wood smoke smell was as elusive as a dream. Sometimes I thought I could smell it, sometimes not. Very faint. A fire could mean people.

I ran the boat ashore and tied it to a small tree where the undergrowth was thick. I stepped away and examined the place where the boat was secreted. Ten feet away, unless you knew the boat was there, branches and undergrowth hid it. I marked the spot inside my brain so I could refind it. As I moved away I marked the spot again. There was a notch in the trees that looked like a canoe.

I moved on, walking upland, away from the river. The ground was wet and a little soft. Even with the pullover rubbers I wasn't shoed for hiking, but the running had made me very leg- and lung-strong and I moved easily enough through the soggy brush and woods.

Fifty yards upland I crossed a dirt road. There was a little gravel on it, but not much. I stood in the middle of the road and listened for a moment. Nothing.

After I crossed the road, I first lost sight and then sound of the swift Blue River.

I was about to turn back when I spied a handkerchief tied to a tree. I went to the white square. There seemed to be nothing around it warranting its being there. It was tied to a thin lower limb of a huge, ancient oak and it fluttered forlornly in the snow wind. I thought it was something my searchers had left for me, perhaps not enough to mention on the telephone, but something that had interested them enough to mark.

I examined the tree more closely and saw why someone had tied a handkerchief to it. There were two pieces of wood nailed to the far side of the tree, one about three feet up the tree trunk, one about the same distance higher. By climbing up the two, I could grasp the first substantial limb of the tree and, from there, make my way on up. I did it. The snow was not yet enough of an impediment to keep me from climbing, still more wet-slick than icy-slick. But the weather was deteriorating.

A few limbs up and I could see the river again. *A place for watching? Or maybe a kid's hideaway?*

The pieces of wood seemed substantial, but old. The nails were rusted, as if they'd been in place on the tree for a long time. That didn't mean much. New or old, they could be something Avery Benjamin or his boys or his ex-wife Cherry had erected. Or anyone else, for that matter. Kids, campers, picnickers.

I climbed back down and circled the tree, moving farther and farther out with each circle, looking for something, anything. If there was a lookout spot, then there had to be a camping spot nearby.

Maybe, if it hadn't been for the accumulating snow, or if the snow had been deeper, I'd never have seen a thing. But the snow was coming down and was sticking here and there, leaving bald patches in some areas and accumulating in others. I came to a place a hundred yards from the tree with climbing steps, a place where the ground was level. I walked over the area looking up into other trees, searching the ground. I did it warily and quietly, not sure, because of the wood-smoke smell, that I was alone.

It was the earth itself that gave the hiding place away. There were lines on the ground where the snow had melted and/or failed to stick, root areas of the trees, places where the undergrowth kept the snow from touching. I could see the earth. The lines were all mixed up from the wind and from the fast-falling, wet snow, but there was one area that was regular rather than irregular. It was a square shape in the earth, devoid of snow.

Like a door in the ground.

I went to the door area and cautiously felt around it, running my finger along the four almost invisible lines in the earth that made a rectangle which seemed almost a perfect square. At one place I found I could fit my whole hand into the earth. There was metal down there. I scraped and dug with my gloved hand and brought up a ring of rusty metal hooked to a frame beneath.

Someplace, not too far away, I thought I heard something and I stopped all movement. I waited and listened. I knelt quietly for a long time with the metal ring in my hand, ready to run.

Nerves.

I began again when the sound did not recur. I pulled at the metal ring, standing to the side. I pulled hard. A door covered with sod came up and I could see down into a hiding hole in the earth itself, a man-made hole. Down below I could see a single dirty sleeping bag. It was spread out by a small stove. The chimney pipe for that went into the earth at the side of the hole and I couldn't see where it exited. The hole was perhaps seven feet deep and about eight feet by eight feet, the side walls tamped hard and strengthened with boards. There were rude shelves along one wall and some provisions stored there, tinned things, and crackers in plastic. Two Cutty Sark scotch bottles, filled with liquid, sat on a higher shelf.

The door was cunningly sprung on some kind of a counterweight. When I raised it to about a ninety-degree angle it slowed and caught and was hard to push.

No one was in the hole. It was neat and orderly inside.

I looked around again, somehow expecting to see Avery Benjamin grinning at me from behind a tree. But there was no one watching.

There was a rude ladder along one side. I went down into the hole and first felt the stove. It was warm. I opened its door and could see a little spark still left when I stirred the ashes with a gloved finger. I thought maybe the stove was the source of the wood-smoke smell.

Someone had been in this place very recently.

I searched some more. On one of the shelves, under a can, I found a written note. It read: "beans, peas, dried meat, aspirin, cigarettes, Bourbon." The words were scribbled. I put it in my pocket. I opened one of the Cutty Sark bottles and smelled the contents. The bottle was now filled with gasoline. The other had a less strong smell. Coal oil, kerosene.

On another shelf, under a tarpaulin, I found some peculiar things. There were five of them, all made alike. A small candle was stuck firmly to a piece of light wood so that it sat upright like a candle on a birthday cake. Glued to the candle, an inch or so below its top, were long, wax-soaked wicks, four of them, each about a foot long. The devices were well made. I put one of the gadgets in my coat pocket and covered the others back up and went on looking. There seemed to be nothing else.

But I knew someone had been here. And recently. That made me doubly wary.

Another far-off sound made me look up and out of the hole. Nothing to see, but I found myself getting very nervous. This sound had been a rough, loud motor sound, like perhaps a Jeep or some kind of truck. I remembered the road above the river. I went nimbly up the ladder and closed the door carefully.

The snow was getting heavier and I smoothed a little of it around the crack lines to try to hide the fact I'd made entry. All I managed to do was make mud lines. Maybe the fast-falling snow would do a better job for me.

I took one last look around to make certain I could refind the place and thought I could. I'd survived before by following my instincts and they told me to get away from this place. It was desolate and lonely and anything could happen to me here.

I moved upland and away from the river, figuring that if someone was coming they'd probably be coming from the road on the river side. I'd found something to tell about and now the task was going to be in getting back across the river to tell about it. Maybe there was someone out there in the woods, maybe not. But the stove had been warm.

I went straight upland a couple of hundred yards, then went downriver at right angles for maybe a mile. I saw nothing, but I did hear the motor sound again, rising and then fading. That spooked me more than open pursuit would have. Someone was out there. I knew it. I stayed behind trees and in brush as much as I could. I felt tense and expectant, as if I was awaiting a slug in the back.

The motor sounds stopped. Once I heard a faraway cracking sound and something whined through the branches of a tree beside me. Maybe it was a shot, maybe not, but it galvanized me into a quick response.

From a long way away, I began to run back to the river. If

someone was watching and waiting, the running would be expected, but not the speed I managed. Here and there I left heavy tracks. I was noisy. If I had a follower, then they could track me back to my boat, but they'd have to do it very quickly because I ran fast in the slippery woods, picking my path, avoiding places where I'd have to slow. Once or twice I almost went down when I hit a slick spot. But I kept going, moving quickly. Another runner might have kept pace, but it would take one in training.

The motor sound came again, this time frighteningly close. Whoever was behind me had gone back to their vehicle. The sound drew nearer.

I crossed the road in a crouch, remembering an old war.

I increased my speed to a flat-out run and watched for the landmarks I'd noted. I almost turned at the wrong one, but saw my mistake and saw the right canoe one nearby.

I found my boat undisturbed, got the motor started after two desperate pulls, and headed for the far bank. My motor sound drowned out anything behind me. When I was thirty feet out into the river I was almost lost in the snow. Something ticked along the side of the boat and I felt it more than heard it. I leaned over and could see the gash it cut. I revved the boat motor full speed. Something whined off the river behind me, but now I was out of range and sight. Any shot that hit me would be a chance shot.

On the nuclear-plant side of the river I set the motor a little lower and headed back upriver.

If there was anyone behind me I didn't see them or hear anything else from them once I was upriver. The small gash in the side of the boat was a reminder that it had been close and it made me shiver as I inspected it.

The old man who'd rented me the boat grunted when he saw the gash, but didn't attempt to charge me for it. I got into Jo's car and drove into snow that was now sticking to both ground and road. A gray sky above indicated that it might be a continuing thing. Twice I had to pull off the road and wait awhile for it to slack up so I could see enough of the road ahead to drive.

Corporal Robert Cadwell wasn't on post, but a curious radioman examined my bedraggled appearance and decided to call him. I waited. Cadwell came in when I was getting warm enough to want to start peeling out of my wet clothes.

He looked me over. My coat was dirty and wrinkled, my feet were muddy, and I supposed I didn't look exactly like the same person he'd seen earlier. My appearance had been what intrigued the radio operator also.

Cadwell grinned. "You look like you been lost for a week in the big woods."

I nodded. "Something like that, but not that long." I reached in my pocket and brought out the device and the note I'd taken from the hiding hole.

He tensed a little when he was examining the device. The note he shoved aside, much more interested in the candle apparatus.

"Do you have a handwriting expert around?" I asked.

"On call, but not immediately available."

"How about someone in the local bank? Someone who'd know Avery Benjamin's writing and could give a curbstone opinion as to whether or not this was in that writing?"

He picked the note up with more interest. "Maybe I could find someone like that. The Drewville bank got taken over last year in a merger with some out-of-town bank, but some of the people who knew Avery are still working there."

"Would you do it?"

"Maybe. I need to know more than that. Where'd the note come from?"

"From a hole in the ground across the Blue River. I guess you'd call it a hiding hole. I used to dig things like it when I was a kid, but not as elaborate as this one. Got a stove in it and some provisions and a bottle of gasoline and another of kerosene. That's where that candle thing came from also." I watched him pick up the device and look at it again. "What is it?"

"I don't know for sure, but my guess would be some kind of fuse. I've seen what was left of something like it. It came out of a house that caught on fire. A house the Drewville Volunteers got to before it burned down. The fireman who found it don't like the sheriff, so he brought it here first." He held the device out so I could see it. "Maybe put it in a coffee can of water with the wicks over the side. Light the candle. The wood keeps it afloat. The candle burns down and the wicks light and run down to something else—gasoline, coal oil, something—below the water in a larger container. We photographed it and then gave it to the state fire marshal." He examined the device fondly. "Was this the only one?"

"There were four others."

He gave me a skeptical look. "It's possible the place you found could have been there for years."

"Maybe. The little stove in the hole still had some embers in it. There was a single sleeping bag. And someone shot at me when I was moving out."

"How do I know you didn't discover all this just to help your partners' case in court?" He smiled, taking some of the sting away. "I've heard all over town you Bington lawyers ain't to be trusted."

"My partners don't need any help. Tomorrow they can get a mistrial and start this all over months or years from now. Maybe in another county, for sure before a new judge. With all the witnesses allowed to testify."

"Is that the way of it?"

I nodded.

"What do you know about Drewville?" he asked.

"Not much. Small town. Lots of people seem related."

"They are. This county is mostly farmers and small merchants. They're the kind of people who tend the land and maybe poach a deer in the fall. Good folks mostly. Avery Benjamin was one of them. He made some money, but I never saw him dressed up in a suit."

"What's that mean?"

"It means it's kind of a blood county. And you're not of the blood. You came in here and things have been happening since."

"Shouldn't I have done what I've done?"

He shrugged. "I'm not saying that. You are."

"I just don't know where you're coming from. This county had its problems long before I got here."

He watched me. "I'll give you an example, Robak. I heard some traffic over the sheriff's radio. Something about someone breaking into Hilda Benjamin's place last night. Someone dug up some spots in her yard and maybe got inside the house."

"I hadn't heard that," I answered stolidly.

"Sheriff had all his deputies checking around there. I heard your name a couple of times. Someone was going to find out where you were staying and check a ladder and spade you bought at Benjamin's." Something about that made him turn his face away from mine so I couldn't read his expression. "Did you buy a ladder and spade from the Benjamin boys?"

I smiled sunnily. "Yes. They've got a lot of nice stuff in that old redneck store."

"Some old man at your motel one county north sent the deputies back for a search warrant," Cadwell said. "Wouldn't let them in and said if they came in he'd law them." He looked back at me. He wasn't really smiling, but the crow's feet at his eye corners had deepened a bit.

"That might be my partner Steinmetz. He's a stickler for the right papers. Used to be the circuit judge down at Bington. It's redneck country too."

"I thought maybe you might want to know they were looking around at your motel."

"Thank you." I shrugged. "If I'd have been there they could have looked without a warrant." I gave him my best sincere look. "I need that ladder and spade at home."

"Maybe you do, maybe not. I wouldn't want to pull them Benjamin boys' tails too much. They're the worst we got around here. When someone ventures an opinion about someone doing something wrong, why, then their names usually get mentioned. They're a couple of mean lads. When they were growing up, Poppa had the money and means to get them out of about anything, and he spent a lot of time and effort and bucks doing just that. He needed to or they'd have spent a ton of time in jail." He thought for a moment. "You want to show me your hole in the ground?"

"If you want. Is what you're saying that I ought to be careful?"

"Yes, and I want." He nodded. "We'll go past my house and pick up my boat." He thought for a moment. "And my rifle."

I thought of a couple of other things. "You told me that your lawyer friend who went off the hill drank scotch?"

"Ray Lucas? Cutty Sark."

"Couple of empty scotch bottles on the shelf in the hiding hole," I said. "Like I said, I smelled inside them. One had gasoline in it now, the other kerosene. Cutty Sark bottles. Now, tell me something? When Ray Lucas was alive and running around, who was he chasing?"

"Mrs. Benjamin. Cherry Benjamin."

I gave him a perplexed look. "I'd have thought it'd be Hilda."

"No. It was Cherry."

"Hilda comes from up around Jewell City. Could you check around up there and see if they're missing a male, about one hundred fifty pounds, no teeth, and maybe five nine or ten? Gone about two years now."

He got up. "Yes, I could do that, but later. Let's go."

We tried. We got across the river and beached his boat close to where I thought I'd tied mine earlier.

By the time we were there the snow was four or five inches deep and it had grown very cold. The wind was drifting the snow. The whiteness changed the land. I found the road, but had no idea where I'd gone above it, how far, what direction. I couldn't tell one tree from the other because the snow was blowing into my eyes, beginning to drift, clinging to trees.

We searched for a couple of hours, but I couldn't find the tree with the handkerchief and I couldn't find any tree that even resembled it.

The snow kept coming down. At times it would be snowing so hard that if Cadwell got a few feet ahead he'd become a shadow.

We gave it up.

Cadwell let me out at my snow-covered car parked in the state police post parking area.

"Never you mind," he said. "This won't last forever. It's supposed to warm up tomorrow or the next day. When the snow gets off, do you think you can find the place again?"

"I think so."

"In the meantime I'll check out the food note and see if anyone can tell me it's in Avery Benjamin's writing." He gave me a keen look. "What good would it do you if it was?"

"No good at all for evidence because there's no way of dating the note. But for my own satisfaction it might do a great deal of good."

"How's that?"

"Like I said, the stove was warm. Maybe Avery Benjamin is also. Or at least not as cold as his lawyer and family would like

him to be. And someone didn't want me in that hidey-hole
and didn't want me telling about it. And don't forget about
Jewell City."

"If I do all this, will you buy me a toy?"

CHAPTER ELEVEN

Sam King's Football Advice: "Never celebrate a victory until you're dead sure it can't turn into defeat. If you don't believe me, let me tell you about my last Purdue game."

I drove back to our motel and found a party of sorts in session. Two insurance company representatives lounged with Sam and Jake and Steinmetz around a square table in the "sitting room" of our motel suite. I'd seen them both around the courtroom, assessing our chances, wise money men who dealt in big dollars. Now they wore smiles under large cigars and one of them was definitely a bit intoxicated, the other aiming that way. There was an empty bottle of champagne in an ice bucket, there were bottles of V.O. and Early Times on the table. There were various bottles of mix, and sacks and cans of Eagle Brand peanut and pretzel snacks, probably purchased in the motel gift shop. Someone had opened a pack of playing cards, but they'd apparently not been used as they lay, face up, with the two jokers still in place and the suits in order. All on the expense account, of course.

"What ho," Steinmetz said from his chair. "Detective O'Robak returneth." He eyed me owlishly. "Do you know our good friends and clients from the insurance industry?"

I nodded at the two insurance executives. I really have little faith and trust in insurance people. Maybe the product they provide is necessary, but they do build a lot of fifty-story office buildings and pay good salaries and high expenses to a lot of people to provide their service. And once an insurance company had canceled me when it had to pay out a thousand-dollar claim (after I'd paid the company some ten thousand in premiums over ten years). Peculiar people.

"I return from the wars and the river," I answered lightly, not wanting to cause problems right off by attacking our employers of the day. Although I didn't like them they were paying us—Jake and Sam, anyway.

Steinmetz considered me from afar. "A sheriff's deputy from Drew County came earlier and wanted to search the premises. He also was seeking you. When I informed him he had no jurisdiction here in this county and asked him to show me a search warrant, he heatedly threatened to haul me back to the Drew County jail. Fortunately for me, that was before Jess Yanack decided to go back north." Steinmetz smiled. "Yanack told him that if he overstepped his authority the state police would pick him up before he made the Drew County line. The deputy, being outgunned, went out to talk on his car radio and get instructions from his God and that's the last we've seen of him." He smiled. "We thought maybe he might wait and waylay you in the parking lot. In fact, we were looking forward to it."

"Didn't see anything of him," I said. "How'd you manage to get Yanack here?" I asked curiously. "He sure slowed Judge Keeler to a crawl."

"An old friend of an old friend. Sometimes one can call in a marker. I've a few left." He drank from his drink and lost interest in me momentarily, perhaps remembering something from the past. He had a memory I'd never seen surpassed, but sometimes it burned and hurt him inside and I'd seen him grow silent before when all seemed well.

Another of my partners took up the Robak hunt.

"What they wanted was to examine your spade and ladder," Jake said carefully. He examined me as if I were a bug under his microscope. "The deputy said they'd return, but I doubt that Judge Keeler will be signing many search warrants on this rather dark day in his life. At least to search rooms this law firm occupies." He nodded at the bottles on the table. "Come sit. Fix yourself a drink." He eyed my muddy coat and pants critically. "Or better, clean yourself up."

"Is that an order from the Drew County judge?"

"More like the board of health. Your ladder and spade are still safe under your bed. I assume you've not found Avery Benjamin?" His voice had become polite and I saw they were all watching me, drinking suspended for the moment, humoring the useful, but odd personage I was.

I shook my head. "Haven't located him yet. You could have let the deputy in to look at whatever I have here as far as I'm concerned."

Steinmetz interrupted: "One does not yield to tyranny." He took another long drink from a dark tan concoction. "Unless one must. And several of us noted that the spade blade and the ladder feet seemed conspicuously clean."

Sam laughed. His dark eyes regarded me companionably. One of the insurance guys clapped him on the back. "I remember when you played football, Sam," he rumbled, momentarily in his zeal forgetting the rest of us. "You were something else. I thought you might go pro."

"Bummed up a knee in the Purdue game," Sam said matter-of-factly, as if college games were not worth remembering. I wondered how many nights he'd spent in dreams of what might have been. He had been very, very good; quick and fast and mean. Big-money mean. Now he was just a lawyer. Like me.

I made a light drink of V.O. and water and took it into my room. There I peeled away my grimy clothes and then stood under the hot shower for a while until I felt like I was clean again.

Prolonged silence out in the center room made me return

there, wearing a towel. Only Steinmetz remained. He was
watching television with the sound turned completely down,
eyes glued to the picture.

"I know," I said. "You squeezed and used the rest of them
for mix."

He smiled. "I let them go on to the dining room. We're to
join them. I wanted a word in private with you before we did
join them."

I finished my drink and poured a wee one into the tiny ice
cube remains inside my glass. I waited.

"I won't ask you if you used your ladder and spade in some
fenced-in private yard in Drewville, as the deputy claimed,
because I don't actually want to know. But I've seen you do
things before that were near the edge. Is there a good reason
in this one to do things that could be considered over the
line?"

"Yes, sir. The first reason is that two kids have died in
Drewville fires. The second is that I think that Avery Benjamin might now be dead, but was undoubtedly alive for a long
time after he was supposed to have burned to death. I also
think there's at least a possibility that the lawyer we replaced
for this trial was murdered, put in his car and run down that
lovely and deadly hill that falls into Drewville."

"And you think you know who killed the two kids, Avery
Benjamin, and the lawyer?"

"Not yet. It could have been the two Benjamin brothers,
Avery's sons. Or it could be someone else. But maybe out
there in the cold and snow the killer or killers think I know or
that I might make a good guess." I thought for a moment.
"And now they may know I've got the state police checking
some stuff I found."

He shook his head. "Does having this going on help you?
Does it help us in this case?" I could see he was trying hard to
understand me.

"Sure," I said. "It's almost as good as me actually knowing.

Whoever it is out there's unsure, on the defensive, probably afraid."

He eyed me curiously. "You're an odd specimen, Don. You can be as good at this legal business as you want to be, but instead you continually follow your own star. One day you may die because of it." He lifted his own drink and cleared the dregs. "I worry about both that and the very high chance that someday a disciplinary hearing before one of the strict ones like Yanack will solemnly take away your right to practice and then all of us who know you will be a bit less because of it." He looked at me and waited.

I shrugged. I liked Steinmetz as well as anyone. Sometimes, when he waxed philosophical and had had a lot to drink, I loved him. He had replaced, for me, the father who'd vanished into the smoke and ruin of my early years. But there were things it was better not to tell anyone, things I was unable to share—hunches, deductions, guesses. Some I couldn't share because they were shadowy, some because they sounded silly without the shadows being run in alongside. Steinmetz knew nothing of what I knew in this case. He'd come to help Jake and Sam.

"Ah well," he said gently. "It's prom time. Shall we join the other girls?"

"Let's," I said, smiling. "Is your dance card full?"

Downstairs, in the dining room, the party continued. The room was about full, perhaps because the snowy roads had driven travelers off the interstate.

A trio of old men played soft music from a small bandstand in a far corner of the dining area. Some brave souls danced, one of them wearing overshoes. There was a clatter of silver intermixed with low-voiced conversation. Pleasant.

I sat down at the table. A waitress brought me a menu and I studied it, hungry and thirsty, but an inner excitement I didn't completely understand interfering with that interest.

"How was the road coming back?" Jake asked me.

"Passable. Ice-covered and slick in spots, but passable." I went back to the menu, not really seeing it, thinking about Drewville and Avery Benjamin.

"You know we have no trial tomorrow?" Jake asked, getting through to me again.

"I thought we were supposed to go back in the morning and decide whether or not to take a mistrial?"

"That was the plan. But there was a call from the court bailiff a bit before you got back. The back roads and side streets in Drew County are impassable. The jury can't get back in. So we don't go back until the day after tomorrow. It's supposed to warm up tomorrow and that should clear the roads." He looked around the table. "The consensus among us seems to be that we take our mistrial. Can you think of any cogent reason why we shouldn't?"

"One very good one. We've got a witness named Mark Koontz. He's a farmer and a former county commissioner and he's a good man. He has a strong local following. Without him we'd not have gotten three of our other witnesses. He's sick. I'd guess it's cancer. If he'd die, your case might be back to zero. So, if you accept a mistrial, the first thing we need to do is depose him. And his deposition may not be as good as he'd be in person."

He nodded. "That's a good reason. I'll take it up with our friends from the insurance companies." He leaned closer. "One of them's an executive vice president."

"High-powered devil," I said. "What's he doing hanging around Drewville and butter and egg hackers like us?"

"They send high-powered people when they stand to lose big money." He gave me a look in which there was some affection. "You sure turned this case around. Next time we can list all those witnesses we weren't allowed to really use."

"And next time we might be minus our best four witnesses.

We got the other three because of Mark Koontz. Maybe we'd keep them if he was dead, maybe not. I'd hate to count on it."

He frowned. "It's something to think on." He bent to his own menu. "We'll worry it around more later. You can argue with the insurance boys."

"You argue with them for me. I think I might want to run back to Drewville tonight. Ask a few questions. Some things about this case bug the hell out of me. Plus I owe some kids some money. I'm running a bit short. Can we get a little money from your insurance bigwigs?"

He nodded. "Sure. You wouldn't be taking your ladder and spade, would you?" he asked diffidently.

I shook my head. "No. That's for home. I need those things there."

"Sure you do. That deputy said someone tore the hell out of Hilda Benjamin's yard digging holes. He said she got damn near hysterical when she saw it. He called her a poor old lady."

"Don't feel sorry for her," I said. "Every day when she comes to court she's a wolf in sheep's clothes."

"How do you mean?"

"I doubt she knows what the Bible she reads is for, and the clothes she wears in court aren't like what she wears to lounge in. And my bet is that she and the sheriff are lovers. If not, they like to play games in a dark house late at night."

"How do you know?"

I described the scene at Hilda's fenced-in house the first time I'd gone there. When I got to the part about the kids and the sheriff, Jake started to grin.

"You really bloodied his arrogant nose?"

"That's me. Old rough-and-ready Robak." I thought for a moment. "For some reason he doesn't like me poking around."

"That's never stopped you before."

"True. I've become acquainted with the local chief of police. He thinks the sheriff is sure he's right in stopping me and/or stomping me. After all, he's the duly elected sheriff of Drew County, and I'm a damned out-of-county interloper. Sometimes I don't understand the peace officer mentality."

"Who does?" he asked sympathetically.

I remembered something. "You were asking questions of someone about Avery Benjamin's sense of humor. Why were you asking those questions? What have we got on that?"

"He was a great practical joker. He'd do anything to get the best of people he knew. He sent out gag valentines long after that went out of style. He pulled elaborate jokes. Once, a few years before he vanished from sight this time, he vanished as a joke. He was gone for a month, right in the middle of his busy season for road construction."

"Where'd he go?"

"When his first wife was still on our side, she said he went to the West Coast. San Francisco, then Los Angeles. She knew where he was—or at least she claimed she knew."

"She's into some church now," I said. "I guess it's maybe a way-out sort of religion." I thought about her on the witness stand and shook my head. "She's really got it bad for that church."

The waitress came and I ordered a small steak and a salad and a tall V.O. and water. I sat there oblivious to the conversation around me, thinking about Drew County and the case. It seemed to me that I knew enough for answers, but none occurred.

The service was slow because the dining room was crowded, but the cocktail waitress was diligent. I stayed out of the case discussion, deferring to Jake and Sam. It was, after all, their case. I drank sparingly.

Outside I could see the snow changing to rain and sleet as it grew a bit warmer, then changing back to snow again as the night grew colder and the wind came up.

Someplace in my vision I perceived something out of the

ordinary. There were lights that shone out on the parking area and none shining inward and blinding me. I could see the land beyond the cars where a hill stretched upward. There was movement there. Why would someone be up there, far away? Light glinted on something metallic.

"All right," I said loudly. "Let's get away from the window." I jumped up. The others watched me blankly.

I was a shade late. A shot penetrated the top of the picture window far above our heads and whined on harmlessly. The window was some kind of a double pane. The inner sheath cracked and began to fall toward us. I pushed the table away and tackled Steinmetz and dragged him underneath the table. Glass crashed in shards all around us.

"Shut off the lights," I yelled. "Someone's shooting outside."

The next few moments were chaos. I lived through them. So did everyone else, even though the dining room lights stayed on.

No more shots came.

Lying under the table, tensed and waiting for other shots, something came to me. I thought I knew who was up on that hill. I thought I might know a possible way to catch that person if I could get Jake and Sam and Steinmetz and the insurance companies to go along.

I wasn't sure, but it seemed worth the chance.

After a while, when the state police had come and gone, after things had settled down and I'd had something to eat, I managed to get away from the insurance men and my partners. I wanted one more look around in Drewville. I wanted to stop and talk to Cherry Benjamin and I wanted to see Ted Powers and maybe some of the other kids he'd hire. But mostly I wanted to talk to Cherry.

Driving back to Drewville was harrowing. It had begun to snow again as the temperature, which had been rising, fell in the dark. There was not much traffic. When another car approached from the other direction the trick was to make enough room on the snow-covered highway for both cars.

I made it without major problems. I drove directly to the Burger King and got myself a cup of black coffee in a plastic container.

I'd barely slid into my booth before Ted Powers appeared. He smiled down at me and sat on the other side of the booth.

"You owe us forty bucks for watching old Mrs. Benjamin hanging around a very weird church. You owe us a hundred more for our trip across the river." He sat uneasily, waiting, perhaps not as sure of me as once he'd been. Even in clean clothes I still had had to wear my muddy raincoat and I surely looked tacky. Not a figure of trust.

I got out my billfold, which the insurance company boys had helped refill. That brought a smile. I counted out three hundred and forty bucks and pushed it across the table to him. He picked it up.

"You're way long," he protested.

"What you did was worth the add-ons. Figure the added two hundred as extra money for the guys who helped on the river. Someone tied a handkerchief back by a tree and that made a difference."

"I did that." He leaned back in the booth and ran a hand through his dark, crisp hair. "On account of the steps up into the tree. I didn't see anything else." He counted the money again. "This is more money than a lot of our guys see in a year. Thanks, Mr. Robak." He gave me an odd look. "I can smell some booze on your breath. Better not let the sheriff catch you. And if anyone tells you that you look good they're telling you a lie."

"Let's hope the sweet sheriff doesn't apprehend me. I had a couple of very light drinks an hour or so ago. I could pass a drunkometer, but maybe not if it was run by the Drew

County Sheriff's Department. And I got my coat dirty-looking around that place you hung the hankie."

He smiled and nodded. Two girls came in the door to the restaurant. His eyes brightened when he saw them.

"Go ahead," I said.

He slid to the edge of the booth. "I got to go and distribute this. You want anything else?"

"Not now. If anyone sees anything or hears anything I ought to know, then I hope you'll get in touch. Did whoever watched Cherry Benjamin say anything about it?"

"Just that she went to this church last night and that he snuck up on it and listened. He said there were a lot of cars and a lot of people and a preacher who never said anything below a shout. He said some of the people put on chains and some took whips and whipped themselves. He got scared they'd see him and he went back to where he'd been—where he could see Mrs. Benjamin's car. He said she was there all evening and was one of the last to leave." He smiled restlessly, still looking at the girls who'd come in. One of them was watching him pointedly. "He said if he had his way, it'd not be the church of his choice."

I leaned a little toward him, ignoring his humor. "I've not been around here long enough to know everything, but I can tell you one thing you should maybe pass on."

"What would that be?" he asked.

"You kids don't like your sheriff. You ought to add on your judge. From what I've seen, the two of them are close—very close."

"We know that. Some of us are going to work at the polls next week. And we've done some talking here and there."

"All right. Go chase girls," I said.

"What?" he asked, startled. He saw my smile and nodded. "Yeah. Sure. Girls." He held out a hand and I shook it.

"I sure thought you was weird that first time I saw you," he said and shook his head.

"I haven't changed."

He nodded agreement and went from my booth to their booth. I watched for a while while I finished my coffee. The crowd grew around Ted Powers's new booth, girls and boys together. Some kids are natural-born leaders. I felt good for him.

I drove past Cherry Benjamin's house. Either the road to the church was snow-blocked or she'd come home early. There was a light on and the old Jeep station wagon was in the drive. I parked. I made my way through the snow and felt the hood of the Jeep. It wasn't cold, but it wasn't hot either. Warm.

I knocked on her door.

She came in a while. She was dressed in an old housecoat and her hair was up in curlers. She opened the door, saw it was me, and blocked it.

"What do you want?" she asked carefully.

"I want to know why you told my partners one thing early and then said another on the witness stand."

She sniffed. "You've been drinking. I'll pray for you because of that. I told them one thing and testified to another because I was sworn to tell the truth the second time. The Lord's told me to tell the truth and tell it I will. Just like it is. I don't owe your insurance companies anything. I do owe my boys."

"Is the truth the fact Avery Benjamin's dead?" I asked sarcastically.

"He's dead," she said, her voice sure. "Now leave here and don't bother me no more." She smiled without humor. "Else I'll set the sheriff on you. I hear he'd like that."

"That wouldn't be Christian," I said.

"Don't fun me on religion," she said seriously. "What I do is what I do. I make the decisions. Don't bother me again."

It was no night to get into a confrontation with the sheriff. She'd shut the door firmly before I was off the porch.

I made one pass around the Benjamin Construction Company compound. Some of the equipment seemed to be gone, some of it had been moved inside. A big door to a storage barn stood slightly ajar. It was dark inside. So was the office. It looked as if no one was around. I resisted the urge to try to get in and look around. I didn't have my ladder and I didn't have the desire—not tonight. Besides, the roofs of the buildings were so covered with thick snow and ice that I could hear the roofs groan as I drove past.

I started the drive back to the twenty-mile motel.

One more V.O. and water and eight hours of sleep.

CHAPTER TWELVE

Jake's Question: "Robak, at your age, why don't you act your age?"

They grabbed me on my way back to the motel. If I'd been alert and observant, maybe it wouldn't have happened, but that wasn't the way of it. I was fighting the snow and ice and trying to drive through it instead of looking out for predators who might be seeking me.

Later that night, when things were going poorly for me, I decided they'd perhaps watched me visit the Burger King, drive past Cherry's, and around their snow-covered compound, then stalked me when I'd not entered that trap.

When I started back to the motel, the road north out of Drewville wasn't impassable, but it was covered again with thick new snow. As the night wore on, if temperatures plunged, it might be impassable until tomorrow's predicted warming unless the county used snowplows and sand and salt on it. But when I started back north, the best single word to describe it was "treacherous."

I drove up the highway cautiously, fifteen to twenty miles an hour. There was no traffic. Drew County, at ten o'clock at night, seemed to be in total hibernation. Now and then my back wheels would spin on the ice or I'd skid a little, but at fifteen-plus miles an hour I was in no danger.

A mile north of Drewville I fell in behind a lone snowplow, which was taking the top crust of snow off the road in a single lane, moving slowly and majestically up the middle of the road so that there was no easy place for a following car to pass. The man driving the snowplow seemed intent on his work, hunched over in his unlighted cab, absorbed in following his own lights up the road. I saw him look once into his rearview mirror and then ignore me. We moved slowly together north on the road at about ten miles an hour, with him spitting out a cloud of snow and me following in the tracks he made. At least he made the road safer.

Behind me, in my own mirror, I saw the lights of another vehicle coming up on me and so I turned on my emergency blinkers. The vehicle, when it was close enough for me to see, turned out to be a pickup truck. The driver liked his brights and kept them on me until I turned the mirror away so that they weren't reflecting in my face.

We then proceeded north for a time, a chain of three. I turned on the radio, found an area station, and learned we were still under a heavy snow warning and that the state police were urging everyone to stay home, and that roads ranged from slick and hazardous to impassable. The interstate north had been closed to traffic, but I figured I could get to my motel. The radio predicted warming by morning, with temperatures into the low fifties by late afternoon.

Moving slowly lulled me. The radio played music, the truck behind me kept on its bright lights, and all seemed well until we were maybe five miles north of Drewville.

I came back to awareness when the man on the snowplow ahead of me stood up in his glass cockpit, turned the vehicle so the road was completely blocked, and braked to a halt. The truck behind me pulled close and bumped me lightly. I noticed something I should have noticed before, even in the darkness. Both the truck and the snowplow were painted a bright Benjamin red.

The snowplow's motor was turned off. The truck behind me also was silent.

I was caught in between the pair.

I did one defensive thing. I took the keys out of the Plymouth and tossed them out into the heavy roadside snow. I then rolled the window back up and locked the doors. Maybe that would hold them for a moment or two, until some other traffic came up to us.

I waited, hunched in the seat. One Benjamin brother got out of the snowplow, the other out of the pickup truck.

Fritz, the one with the yellow eyes, came to my car door. He motioned me out.

He smiled and shouted. "Won't nobody be along, Robak. No use for you to tarry. I blocked the road back a ways. Get out easy or we'll smash in your windows."

I waited. He went back to his truck and came back with a spade much like I'd bought from the store.

"Out," he ordered. "Else I take this to you once I get you out."

I nodded my surrender and opened up the car door. I got out. I acted cowed and afraid and nervous. I was all three.

The other brother was off his snowplow. He came walking cockily toward me.

"Move his car off the road," he ordered Fritz.

Fritz opened the door of Jo's car and looked back at me. "Keys," he ordered.

"I threw them away," I mumbled.

Fritz nodded at Eric. "He did throw something out the window. I seen him."

Eric looked at me. "Wise bastard." He turned to Fritz. "Get the ropes and we'll tie Mr. Shyster Smart-Ass up." He produced a large, shiny revolver. "I hear you can run. You try to run and I'll blow a hole in you, shyster man. We get you trussed up and under a tarp in the truck, then we'll hot-wire your car and run it off the road where no one'll find it for a while. Long enough for us and you, anyways."

"Long enough to do what?" I asked.

"You'll see." He smiled, thinking about it.

I waited. Rough hands wound ropes over and around me, concentrating on wrists and ankles. I tensed my muscles as much as I could. I listened to see if I could hear any traffic approaching, but there was nothing. The only sound was the wind. Perhaps they had blocked the road.

"What'd you tell that state cop? Why'd he get his boat and long gun and go across the river with you this afternoon?" Eric asked.

"We just took a little hike together." I remembered a Robert Frost poem. "To see the woods fill up with snow. Maybe to build us a snowman or a snow fort. He and I are both into winter sports." I shook my head. "Why are you bothering with me? Your lawsuit's already dead. Judge Keeler's going to grant a motion for a mistrial day after tomorrow."

"Maybe he is, maybe he ain't. Our lawyer don't know for sure what's going to happen. No one on your side's saying, and that guy from upstate has gone. Maybe we get rid of you and things will change back again. The law don't like to fool with us in this town." He smiled. "We're bad. Real bad."

"Your big lawsuit's dead," I said. "Day after tomorrow there'll either be a mistrial declared or you'll lose."

"You won't be there to see it noways. You caused us problems, Robak. Me and Fritz always pays back. You should have asked around. Anyone around Drewville would have told you that. So we made some good plans for you. You should have stayed in your own town and kept your long nose out of our business. When people mess in our affairs, we teach them." He smiled at me as if anxious to hear my reaction.

I looked them over. They were large and strong and not very bright. "What happened to your father?" I asked curiously.

"We'll talk back at the compound." He inspected my ropes by yanking on them as a cowboy would with a trussed-up steer. They were tight enough to satisfy him. I stood upright in the middle of the snow-covered highway like a mummy.

He strongly lifted me up and tossed me casually into the back of the pickup truck. He did it almost effortlessly. The truck had one of those topper covers over the bed and it was warmer inside than outside, but not much. Eric hopped up after me and stuffed paper tissues in my mouth until I almost gagged on them. Then he covered me with a tarp that smelled strongly of paint and dust and something else far more foul. He whacked me once with the spade in my mid-section, a hard blow. It hurt enough to bring tears to my eyes. I coughed a couple of times into the tissue and it hurt when I coughed. I willed the coughing to stop and it did.

I heard him get out and the tailgate door close.

It was dark under the filthy tarp and I had the urge to sneeze. When I did sneeze it felt like something would tear loose inside me. I fought it and won temporarily.

I heard Jo's Plymouth start after a while.

The tailgate-type door into the covered area of the pickup truck opened once more and I could feel eyes on me. I lay quietly.

My watcher laughed once and the door closed again.

I went to work on the ropes, but there seemed to be nothing I could do. They were heavy and tight around me. I could move inside them a little, but couldn't get leverage on them, could find no place to work on them. They were bulky and strong.

We were moving.

I did manage to get close enough to the side of the truck to bang my head and feet against the walls, but I could hardly hear the result.

We stopped moving after a while.

All was quiet. The tailgate door opened once more and I could feel eyes on me. Someone pulled the tarp down a little and I breathed fresher air.

"Wouldn't want you to smother. We got other plans for

you. Hot times for old Drewville tonight. Volunteer fireman's dream."

The tailgate closed.

By lifting my head as far as I could, I was able to look out the back glass and see a few things. We were in a big garage. Around me I could see red-painted road equipment with "B" on each door. I figured we were in one of the buildings on the Benjamin compound, one where they stored equipment in bad weather. Rusted old equipment sat behind the truck I was in. There was no light inside the building. But a single narrow window directly opposite where I was let in light from outside so that there was dimness, but not dark.

My stomach and chest hurt where I'd been hit by the spade. I found myself flitting in and out of the dimness inside the garage. There didn't seem to be any bleeding, but maybe a rib or two had been cracked or broken. I exacerbated things more by trying to wriggle against the binding ropes, but they seemed impregnable.

After what seemed a long time, the Benjamin boys returned. Fritz dragged me out of the truck bed and let me fall heavily to the asphalt floor. I hit on my head and saw white fire and stars.

He lit a kitchen match and held it in front of my eyes.

"See the fire," he said, watching the tiny flame with his odd eyes. "See the pretty fire." He eyed me curiously. "Do you know who the god of fire is?"

"Watch doing that," Eric said reasonably. "There's enough stuff in this place to blow us all away. And we don't want that to happen yet, Fritz."

Fritz smiled. He put out the match by rubbing it against the side of my face, burning me a little. He jerked the wad of tissues out of my mouth.

"Scream if you want. This place is closed up and there's no one around. Maybe screaming will make you feel like you're doing something."

I stayed silent.

"You'll get yours soon enough," he said darkly. "Now we want to know just exactly what you told Cadwell today and why you went across the river with him and were over there for a couple of hours. And how come you keep going around where all them goofy kids are? Why do you do that, Robak?"

"Naturalists," I said. "Cadwell and me are into nature studies. I've known him for years. We wanted to see if it was snowing over there like it was snowing here." I smiled up at them. "It was, too. I was going to take the kids on a hike with us."

"Can I light another match?" Fritz begged Eric. He eyed me with desire apparent in his yellow eyes. "Just for him?"

Eric shook his head. "Not now, Fritz. But soon. We'll get things set to go real soon now." He kicked me hard in the hip. "Someone got into Pop's old dugout today. We know that. We think it was just you, but maybe it was you and Cadwell."

"What happened to your father, Avery Benjamin?"

Eric smiled down at me. "He burned up in a fire a couple of years back."

"No. I know that's not so."

"How do you know it?" Eric asked, interested.

"Too many people saw him afterward, even if you did threaten most of them into saying they didn't. He was around up to a month or six weeks back. I don't think he's around now."

"Pop's still someplace," Eric said confidently. "This thing gets over, he'll show up again. Or he'll let us know where he is. He'll need money. This way he's away from all those federal people who were bothering him."

"I wonder. I think he's dead now," I said. "I think one of you probably killed him. The question is which one of you did it. Maybe both of you?"

Eric and Fritz looked at each other. Eric shook his head solemnly and then the two of them considered me.

"Pop's alive. Maybe he went to California again. Maybe Canada. He never asked our permission before and he didn't this time either. Your damned insurance companies would like to find him, but they won't. Whether we win the trial now or next year, we'll win it sometime. They owe us. They should have paid us."

"You can't hold out until next year," I said, with a confidence I didn't feel. "All you've got are a bunch of rust buckets you call equipment and a few hundred dollars' worth of stock."

Fritz smiled at Eric. "We also have a plan. You might call it our fire-sale plan. We decided today to make you a part of that plan. And maybe that state cop Cadwell, too."

"Kill me or a state trooper and they'll never stop looking— never."

Fritz kicked me. This time it was lightly, almost affectionately. "Maybe a state cop would cause an uproar, but not you, Robak. Accidental. That's what this bonfire will be. Sheriff knows you were in at Hilda's place, and when they find what's left of you here, they'll just think you were where you oughtn't to have been again, and that it was all a tragic accident caused by your unlawful entry. You see, there's a lot of gasoline stored here. Sheriff won't look any further. He don't like you anyway. It'll just be another accident."

"What kind of accident?" I asked. "Like the rest you and your brother have caused? Fire accidents?"

"You'll find out," Eric said. "But sure, we set a lot of fires. We set them for people who paid us. We set them on people who got out in the way. It was the only way for us to live when your insurance companies turned us down."

"Did you burn up those kids?"

"One of them. Little bastard. Always whining and in trouble. His parents paid extra for him. Fritz got him quiet and then we set the place on fire. Got three thousand for that one." He shook his head. "The other one, that Gannett kid, must have been accidental." He laughed without humor. "Only fire in Drewville or Drew County in the last two years we didn't set."

"Did you set the one where your father was supposed to have died?"

"No. Maybe that one was accidental, too. Or maybe Pop set it." He lost patience in talking with me. "Now, what did you tell Cadwell?"

I thought on it. They didn't know what I'd seen. They weren't sure I'd been in the hiding hole, only sure I'd located it. I wondered about that.

"I told Cadwell I thought I might have found something in the woods and that someone had shot at me when I was running away. I asked him to go back over the river with me. He did, but we couldn't find anything in all this snow." I gave them my best morose look. "I couldn't even find the tree I took my bearings from."

Eric smiled. "Maybe it is the way you're saying. There's always time to take that state cop out even if he's extra careful. We'll see what he does after he finds out you're dead. Me and Fritz will watch him. We're good at watching and waiting. Eric was watching when you drove past a while ago."

Fritz smiled also. He nodded at Eric. "Go out and see there's no one around."

Eric shrugged. "Everyone's home and safe. All snug and warm." He nodded to me. "Soon you'll be that way too."

Fritz said, "Take a look. Then we'll set the candles and get on to the V.F.W." He smiled down at me. "When this place goes up we'll be having a couple of drinks and maybe playing some cards at the club with half a dozen friends." He nodded his head at the wall. "There's gas in here. There's also half a case of dynamite. I've heard some say it just burns in a fire, but this is dynamite with a fuse, not a cap. Be interesting to find out. Me and Eric didn't have any trouble getting insurance for this place." He smiled. "You see, we've never had a fire here."

Eric went out. I thought about trying to yell when he opened the door, but it opened and closed all in one sound and the crucial time was past.

Fritz lit one more match. I could smell fumes around me in the building, a subtle smell. He held the match down by my face and watched my expression. I concentrated on the tiny flame.

"Who is the god of fire?" he asked again.

I waited, not certain what he'd do, knowing he was insane.

He ground the match out against my cheek, missing my right eye by a fraction. He laughed. Things went dim again for me.

He gave me up and went prowling around the storage building. I saw him set up some small "things," one on a shelf, two others in other areas of the building I could not see. I heard him pouring liquids into containers. I knew he was doing his job in more than the one place I saw because he'd stop and I'd not hear him for a moment, then he'd move on. Trying to watch him let me also see some other things on shelves and hanging on the walls. On shelves there were cans of something or other. I couldn't make out the writing, but I thought they were maybe something to add to hot mix or perhaps yellow paint for stripe lines. Along the wall that was the farthest I could see there were hoes and tampers, rakes and shovels. Alongside them, hung from a peg on the wall, there was a gasoline power saw that looked almost new.

The roof above me groaned and creaked from the great weight of the snow burdening it.

I tried the ropes again. The warmth inside the garage seemed to have loosened them a little. I found I could wiggle my right hand some and that my right leg had a tiny bit of play between it and the ropes so that I could turn it and move it. I pushed and pulled and did the best I could to exploit those areas, but there seemed to be little progress.

I heard Eric come back through the door. I tried a yell, but it didn't seem to alarm either of them. They moved close to me and stood there.

Eric said, "No one around outside. Light up and we'll get out of here." He smiled down at me in the dimness. "You now have about fifteen minutes, Robak. There are some candles. They burn down to a certain place and light some wicks. Those set off kerosene and then gasoline. You'll be warm, but only for a few moments."

"I saw some candle things in the hole," I said, trying to slow things down.

"No matter now," he said. "Light them, Fritz."

Fritz gave me one last kick and I saw him light a candle and heard him light more. In a moment the Benjamin brothers were at the door.

"Hot dreams," Fritz called to me. He closed the door and I thought I could hear him laughing. I yelled once and the echo came back to me. They'd not have left me if yelling would do any good.

With the leg I could move a little and the hand that had some leverage I rolled. It was slow going and took all my effort. I rolled toward the wall and the tools there. I was counting as I rolled, but after a time I gave the counting up. I found I was perspiring heavily. The time passed quickly.

I made it to the tools, but nothing in the bin seemed to have a sharp enough edge to help me. The hoes were dull and covered with asphalt residue.

I slid up against the wall. Three times I fell back, but finally, by falling against a retainer that held the tool bin, I remained upright, still trussed tight, but upright.

I hopped a tiny hop and then another. The power saw was at my back. I turned to it as best I could and rubbed the ropes against the chain. I could feel them cutting a little. I saw the flicker of the candles. I rubbed harder.

Something gave. I had a hand free. I rubbed some more. I had both hands free. There were still ropes around me and there was no time to untie them all. I needed something quicker.

The power saw started on the second pull. I cut ropes and clothes and some flesh. I saw the flame blaze up in one corner.

The ropes fell away and I was free. I flung the power saw through the single window, breaking the glass. There was no time to try for the door. I saw a track of flame running toward me. I dived at the window and was caught in its confines for a second, and then was through, scraped and raw, but whole. I got up from the ground below the window.

I saw a huge puff of flame inside. I started the saw again and cut into a window frame, hoping to bring the roof full of snow down on the fire, but it was too late. There was more flame from the window and I remembered the dynamite and ran. I kept running from the building for much longer than was necessary.

I heard sirens, but I had no trust for them. One of the sirens could be the sheriff. I watched the flames sweep into the sky for a time, consuming at least the one building. I then headed for the state police barracks. I kept to alleys and dark streets. At the edge of town I walked far off the road, fighting the snow.

Eventually, I made it.

CHAPTER THIRTEEN

Statute: "A person who, by use of fire or explosive, know-ingly or intentionally damages the property of any person, with intent to defraud, commits arson."

"They did *what?*" Cadwell asked me. "Now slow yourself down, relax, and go through the whole thing for me once more."

I repeated what I'd already told him and finished by saying "I'm sure the Benjamin brothers think I'm dead, Corporal. Burned to french fries in the fire they set on purpose in their storage building. What I'd like to have you do is get a photographer in here to take some photos of me and then have a doctor check me over. I got kicked some and smacked with a spade and I'm achy and sore, although it seems to be less than I thought it would be and I can still move all right. The blood and the cuts and bruises are from the chain saw and from going through a window that was one size small and took the hide off me in several places. The cuts and bruises don't bother me that much. I'm thankful I've got them. The Benjamin fire is why I'm here and why I'm angry."

"You look like you been through a couple of wars," he said thinly. "The first thing I want to do is get some warrants out for the two Benjamin boys." He shook his head, thinking. "That might be harder than you think, with Damon Lennon sitting over there in court representing them and their step-mother in this lawsuit about Ave."

"Don't even try for warrants yet," I said. "Soon, but not

yet. Not tonight." I held up a hand to stop his reply. "There are a couple of reasons. My personal one is I want to walk into that courtroom day after tomorrow with them there and have them see me and know their dreams and days of defrauding insurance companies are over. And tomorrow my partners will serve subpoenas on them to make sure they are there."

"Be a real good time to pick them up now," he mused. "Damon sees you tonight and maybe he'll buckle in and do the job he was elected to do. Half the town's at that fire along with the Benjamin boys," he said. "That place really went up hot. I could still see some flames when you came dragging in, but it had died down some from when it first started." He smiled without real meaning. "Something about a fire. Draws people."

"I know it's a big fire. I was supposed to be the centerpiece. For a time, the way they talked, you were going to be a special guest also, but they're only watching you for now. They were very interested in us going across the river."

"Me? They never saw the day they could take me."

"They were going to try." I thought for a moment. "I imagine they'll tell the sheriff and the volunteer firemen not to worry, that there couldn't have been anyone in the building. Then, in a week or so, while cleaning up, they'll discover my burned bones." I looked around the redone, old house that was now a state police post. We were in a room of it that was some kind of office. It was drab and dark and not much, but I was glad to be there. Outside the single small window I could hear the wind whistling and the snow was still falling. I'd been cold when I came in, but now I was warm again.

"I'd feel better, was I you, if they was in jail," Cadwell said.

"First things first. We get rid of the case on Avery and then your prosecutor won't have to make any loyalty choices."

He thought about it and finally nodded.

"Do you think you could get someone to smuggle me to my motel later?"

"Sure." He nodded his head. When he moved, the service badges on his uniform rattled a little. "I called your chief of police down there in Bington yesterday. I know him. George Gentrup. He told me you were always causing trouble. I guess he's right." He thought for a long moment, brows furrowed. "He said also that sometimes you do come up with answers, like now. I know you're right and I know one oughtn't to put pressure on a small-town prosecutor-lawyer like Damon Lennon, but I'd still feel better with the Benjamin boys in jail."

"Think on it," I said. "What you've got right now is them saying to me they did some things, nothing specific, just assorted arsons for hire. In one of those a child died. If your prosecutor would call a grand jury and offer some immunity, maybe some of those arson charges would stick. Outside that, all you've got is me as a witness to what happened in their place tonight."

He nodded.

I could see he still was unconvinced. I leaned forward. "What happens to the best arson charge you have, the one you surely can make stick, if you shove them in jail tonight and they smell a rat and never file a claim? What crime do they commit by burning their own place? Maybe it's an ordinance violation, but it's not arson. And you have to tell their lawyer, who is the local prosecutor, what's going on in order to get warrants."

"You mean them setting fire to their place isn't a crime?"

"Not a serious one. Trying to burn me in it is a crime. It's attempted felony murder. But the crime of arson is completed when you burn your own property and then file a claim for it with the insurance in an attempt to defraud them. That makes things peculiar as far as charging them with trying to burn me up. Something would surely stick, but maybe not attempted felony murder. Read the statute."

"So we wait." He sounded convinced.

"Sure. And after you get me checked and photographed and place the chain saw I brought into your evidence room, I plan to spend some time in my motel room's bed. There I can tell my partners about how they're to act about my disappearance."

"What's the purpose of me keeping the chain saw in the evidence room?"

"My guess is that it was the newest thing in that storage building. Someplace in the office they'll have serial numbers for it and they'll use those when they file insurance claims. If I wasn't there when the fire was set, how'd I get the chain saw they'd filed a claim on?" I watched him. I was very tired and I hurt in two dozen places. "Right now, if I claim they tried to murder me or others, I'm a lawyer on the other side of a mean lawsuit against them where they're represented by your local prosecutor, who has dreams of a fat fee. So you give them the time to help hang themselves. The chain saw corroborates my story. The photos you take and the doctor's examination you give me further corroborate my story. And you let the court case on Avery get to a conclusion."

"Okay. I have the post photographer coming. He should be here soon." He leaned closer and examined me. "Your eyebrows are singed a lot. There ain't a whole bunch left up there. If anyone thinks you're pretty, they ought to get examined."

"I'm lucky that things are only singed. Could you maybe make arrangements to pick me up tomorrow and borrow me a police uniform, bandage me up, particularly in the face, and take me some places? I'd like to see some things."

"Robak's Drewville branch office," he mused, but then nodded. "Why is it that I feel like I'm working for you? Your police chief warned me about that sort of thing."

I smiled as if he were telling a joke. "Make sure no one on the post says a thing." I leaned back in my hard chair, fighting sleep.

"Don't go to sleep on me yet, Robak. If you do I'll kick you where it hurts."

"That's everywhere."

He leaned forward. "First time you talked to me we discussed Ray Lucas and his late-night crash down Cemetery Hill. How about him? How about that wreck?"

"Was Lucas recognizable after the crash?"

"Sure. It was Ray all right. His car didn't burn, more's the miracle."

I shook my head. "I don't think the Benjamin brothers did him. Maybe they did, but my guess is no."

"Was it an accident?"

"I don't know. Maybe we'll find out as things progress. I never had anything other than a hunch to make me think it wasn't an accident."

"And you told me to check for any disappearances up around Jewell City a couple of years ago. Why?"

"Hilda Benjamin's from there. Was there such a disappearance?"

He nodded. "I talked to the sheriff up there. It was a courthouse bum. An alcoholic. Weight about one sixty. Height five foot nine. Age sixty. Disappeared the day before Avery Benjamin's place burned down. Name was Alfred Joseph Smith. Sheriff said they never looked very hard for him."

"Any teeth? Any distinguishing marks of any kind?"

"I didn't ask."

"Ask," I said, yawning. I drifted off for a moment.

"Tell me more about this. Tell me what's happening," he said insistently. "There's got to be more to this than burning a few houses for profit."

I shook my head. "I'm not sure on all of it. I may have a way of finding out some more in the courtroom day after tomorrow, if you can keep me alive until then."

He smiled confidently. "I'll keep you alive, Robak. You've got my competitive instinct aroused."

The photographer came before the doctor. I was photographed from more angles than a *Playgirl* model. The doctor came later and did some stitching where I'd cut myself going through the window and some more where I'd been negligent and hasty with the saw. He bound my sore chest tightly with tape. He hemmed and hawed a lot at the bruises and talked about a hospital. When I demurred he painted me up so that I looked like a springtime Girl Scout with both measles and a lot of merit badges. I dozed through the least part of the treatment.

In the morning I slept in late, probably because of the pills the doctor had given me. Steinmetz smuggled me back a glass of orange juice, coffee, and some hard rolls. I gnawed on them for breakfast. Steinmetz told me that energetic workmen were already fixing the dining room window and that there were state police checking things on the hill.

"This case is also all over the area television news. Not much about it, but interesting stuff. Questions about what's going on in Drew County. Should have Amos Keeler squirming."

"That's good," I said.

"Better than good," he said. "It might get Amos beat."

I got out of bed and tried walking and found I could, but I was sore as a new boil. Things that had not hurt the night before now hurt. But my chest was better and I could breathe.

At ten in the morning I had Steinmetz call Sheriff House's office. He inquired stiffly if I was housed there or if they'd perhaps seen me. He described my car. He stopped short of saying I'd not been seen since the night before.

When he was finished and had rehung the phone he grinned at me. "I got the dispatcher, but she recognized your name. She said she'd put the information out and also call the Drewville police. She asked me politely if maybe you might have run off because they were looking for you. No warrant, but she said Sheriff House was anxious to talk with you."

"I don't want to talk to him," I said sourly. "He's about all I'd need after a double dose of the Benjamins."

Jake watched me eat. Steinmetz and Jake claimed Sam had gone for a walk or a run, but I figured he was out watching things. Or maybe trying to make sure I wasn't seen by reporters. That could ruin things some.

"You sure are real banged up," Jake said. "And now you say you want us to subpoena everyone all over again?"

"Subpoena the sheriff, Hilda, Cherry, and the boys. Also call the rest of our witnesses, Mark Koontz and his people and the ones we had in town, whether they've changed their stories or not. All of them. One way or the other, maybe we'll win."

"Am I supposed to question the witnesses?"

"Would it be all right if I started?" I asked. "There won't be that many I'll call. If we need to call more, you can take care of that."

He nodded gloomily. "Whatever you say, but I thought you turned up your long nose at civil cases?"

"This isn't strictly a civil case anymore. Not for me, anyway."

"I'll vote for that," Steinmetz said. He looked me over again. "What's Jo going to say when she sees you? You look like a poorly constructed jigsaw puzzle."

At about ten o'clock, as arranged, Corporal Robert Cadwell came for me. He shook hands limply with my partners. He'd brought me a uniform that was a size large. He'd also brought me a big blue wide-brimmed Stetson trooper hat and some extra bandages to wrap around my face. Sam came in and, having wrapped many an ankle, did the honors, then painted some gooey unguent artistically here and there on the end result.

"You were in a wreck two weeks ago," Cadwell advised me. "Anyone asks anything and you let me do the talking. I don't want you blowing my case." He grinned at me. "I might make sergeant yet."

I nodded meekly. I hobbled after him to his car.

"Where to?"

"Let's go past the Benjamin place first," I muttered through the bandages. I had a couple of eye holes, but no one had cut me much of a mouth. Maybe purposefully. The unguent smelled like dead bodies.

We drove south. It was warm again, maybe into the forties. The road was wet and, here and there, snowy and icy, but it was improving by the minute.

"Short winter," Cadwell commented.

I'd like to have laughed, but laughing hurt.

"I took the note you got out of your hole past a lady I know who works at the bank. She says she's pretty sure it's Avery's writing."

I nodded, unsurprised.

We drove to the Benjamin compound. Inside, small plumes of smoke still arose from the spot where the storage building had been. Twisted piles of steel were the only remains of the road machinery. The truck I'd been dumped and hauled in sat on the rims in the center of what was left of the building. It looked like a vehicle someone had used for a Beirut car bomb. There was no glass left in any of the windows and the rear end was gone, vanished, probably from when the gas tank had gone up. I shivered a little. *Someone was walking on my grave.*

Both Benjamin brothers were in evidence. I saw one of them moving toward us.

"Here comes a problem," I said.

"Shut up. I'll do the talking," Cadwell said. He rolled his window down and smiled out of it.

The brother who approached was Lemon Eyes—Fritz, the one who'd burned me and who'd wanted to know who the god of fire was.

"Mornin', Fritz," Cadwell said from his window. "Hear you had a bad fire."

Fritz leaned down and looked in the car. "It was a baddie, all right. Got most of our equipment. Insurance man's looking around now." He shook his head, still watching me. "We sure have had a lot of bad family luck." His voice was amiable. "Maybe this time we'll get some fair treatment and a fast check."

Cadwell nodded sympathetically. "This here's my cousin, Albert. Works up north. Got hurt in an auto accident. Car burned when he was after someone and there was a tire shot out. First day out of bed for him. He's staying with me and I'm showing him around."

I nodded and mumbled something through the bandages.

Fritz smiled, interested. He wrinkled his nose, probably at my odor. "Car burned, eh? How'd that feel?" His lemon eyes sparkled.

"Hot," I croaked hoarsely.

"Yeah. It would, wouldn't it." He nodded at Cadwell and at me. "Got to get back in. It'll cool off enough inside to dig around in a day or two. Too warm now. Still hot in places."

He went back inside the compound. In a while a man in a suit came and went in also. Cadwell and I watched him conferring with the brothers. The man in the suit had out a pen and a yellow pad. After a while he went into the office-store building with the brothers.

"Bingo," Cadwell said. "I know the guy in the suit. His name's Owen Long. Insurance adjuster. I'll call him tonight and make sure they filed their claims." He started up the car.

"Maybe we ought to move on. Don't want to seem too curious."

"Right."

"Where to then?"

"Drive me past Hilda Benjamin's place."

He nodded.

We drove past at normal speed. Some of the holes I'd dug had been filled. In one area of the side yard there was a deeper hole near one I'd started.

"That hole looks a lot deeper than the others," I said conversationally. "If I was a tax man, I'd say that's the one the mason jars full of money came from."

"What mason jars?" Cadwell asked, not comprehending.

"Forget it. Family joke and unfunny."

No one was in the yard and the sheriff's car wasn't in sight. We drove on.

"How now?" Cadwell asked.

"There's a church. It's called the Redeemer Church. Out in the county someplace. Do you know where it is?"

"I know it. They have trouble there now and then. People trying to get their kids back."

"Let's go past there."

"Awful early for anyone to be there," he said.

"Then we'll go back past later," I said irritably.

"Sure, sure," he soothed. He drove on out to the highway. Now and then we'd pass people going toward town. Most of them waved at Cadwell. He waved back.

The Redeemer Church sat in a hollow off a gravel road. It was an old wooden church. There were a few cars in the parking area next to the church. One of them was the Jeep I'd seen parked in Cherry Benjamin's drive.

"That one there belongs to Cherry Benjamin," I said, nodding at it.

"I know," he said. "I know most of the cars in this county. You want to park and go in?"

I shook my head. "No. Cherry's pretty acute. We go walking in and it might look wrong to her. I'll have another look at her tomorrow."

"How about we park and I just stick my head inside and tell her there's been a missing person filed on you and we're looking for you?"

I thought about it and it seemed all right. "Okay."

He wheeled his cruiser into the lot and parked near the door of the church. He got out and went through the front door, leaving it ajar. I could see in a little. Up front there was a pulpit with a huge cross over it. There was a microphone on the pulpit and a mass of amplifying equipment at one side.

Cherry Benjamin and two other women were dusting and cleaning near the back of the church. She stopped when Cadwell drew near. I could see them talking. She was dressed plainly. So were the other women. They ignored the conversation and went back to work.

In a while Cadwell came out.

"She didn't seem surprised," he said. He gave me a quick look. "If I wasn't sure I was wrong, I'd say she was drinking. I thought I smelled it on her breath."

He started the car. "Where now?"

"Just drive around. No. There's another place I want to see. Can you drive me to where the original Benjamin home was? The one where he was supposed to have died two years or so ago?"

"Sure."

I put my head back and rested. He drove.

The house was off a side road without another house nearby. It lay in ruins. The snow that had covered the blackened remains had already become discolored. I got out of the car and slogged up to the remains. The only remaining portion of the big house left standing was a three-car garage, fallen in on one end but not on the other. I went in there and looked around.

Nothing, but then I'd not expected anything.

Then, in the very center of the garage, there was something. A fire-blackened spot. Nothing had fallen from above and made it. I stood there inspecting it until Cadwell came up. The spot was about ten feet long by maybe eight feet wide. Above it there were marks on the beams of the garage roof. I reached up and touched one. The wood had charred some. The fire had either been very hot or large enough to reach the ceiling.

The concrete floor below was undamaged. It looked to me as if someone, after the fire, had scrubbed it down with something. And someone could also have used water on the roof beams to keep them from burning. There were a couple of cracks in the floor and I bent to examine them. They seemed like the rest of the cracks. Maybe they'd been there for a long time.

"Someone burned something here," I said. "Then they did some cleanup afterward."

He shook his head. "Maybe kids or picnickers. Get cold and come in and set a fire to keep warm. Then worry about getting caught and clean up some. Don't look like it was here when they had the big fire. Looks too recent."

"Recent?" I asked.

"Sure. See how dirty the rest of the floor is? The part where there was a fire's the only part that's been washed."

I looked down again. He was right.

CHAPTER FOURTEEN

Sam's saying: "So far I've learned that a trial has a beginning and an end. What's surprising is what happens in between."

I waited impatiently, slumped deep in the back of Jake's Buick, until right on nine o'clock the next morning. Across the street, Cadwell also waited, along with three other state police officers. Once, as I sat slouched down, Cadwell moved close to the car and said, loudly enough for me to hear, "They filed the claim. All of them signed it. Hilda, too."

"That's sweet," I said and stayed down out of sight.

Jake and Sam had already gone upstairs to the courtroom. I waited about ten minutes and, when activity seemed to have declined, took the elevator up while two state police officers took one set of steps and the other two climbed those at the opposite end of the building so that the five of us would arrive at about the same time.

The subpoenaed witnesses sat and stood in coveys in the hall.

The bandages were off my face and I was wearing the only suit I'd brought with me. I knew I still didn't look very good. My face was raw from burns, and the fire had singed not only my eyebrows but also my hair.

I saw Fritz and Eric before they saw me. They were sitting on a bench in the hall, legs sprawled in front of them, seemingly bored with this legal business. They watched the other witnesses calculatingly, perhaps making a new list for fire frivolities. Large men, strong and mean. Cherry Benjamin, their mother, sat a few feet away from them wearing old clothes and gum boots.

On down the hall I saw Sheriff Brick House lounging against a wall, talking to some county commissioners. He eyed me with surprise. He started to say something, but I brushed on past him.

Mark Koontz nodded to me from another bench. He sat with the three friends I'd talked to at his farmhouse. I smiled at them.

The hallway was crowded with other witnesses and courthouse people who'd sensed something was happening and not wanted to miss it. The young lady who'd ordered me out of the commissioner's office a few days back watched me with scornful, mistrustful eyes.

Water ran in streams down the windows of the old courthouse. It was melting fast outside, forty-plus degrees, soon to be in the fifties. The unseasonable storm was over.

I was almost up to the Benjamin brothers when they spied me. By that time there were state police at each end of the corridor.

"Morning, all," I said cheerfully.

Eric eyed me stoically, but Fritz did a double take. His round yellow eyes widened and then opened and closed nervously. His hand went to his mouth and he pulled at his face with it. He slid back on the bench and snatched his feet from out on the floor to a protected place under the bench, perhaps afraid I'd stomp them.

I leaned a little toward Fritz. "Now you know. I am the god of fire," I whispered without smiling. I waited for a moment to see what that did to him. He turned pale and held up a hand in alarm. I then moved quickly on past Eric and Fritz and entered the courtroom from its back entrance. Outside I heard a little commotion and then a single scream.

"Your honor," Jake said, rising. "This is our legal partner Donald Robak. He'd like to call our next witness."

The courtroom was full. There were a lot of news people I recognized. I heard some murmuring. The news of my disappearance seemed to have spread.

Judge Keeler pursed his lips. Damon Lennon got to his feet.

"Plaintiffs have no objection, your honor," he said bravely. He sat down and Hilda Benjamin, in her court disguise, tapped his arm and he turned to her for conversation. She spoke to him with vigor. I smiled at the two of them.

The jury members eyed me tranquilly, seven of them, six and an alternate. Four women, three men. I'd thought there were only six members before.

Keeler nodded. "All right, but let's get on with it." He looked up at the clock. It was five minutes past nine.

"I'd like to recall Mrs. Cherry Benjamin."

Keeler nodded down to his bailiff. "Get her." He smiled coldly down at me. "Your reputation precedes you, Mr. Robak."

I inclined my head and smiled back. I doubted we'd have severe problems with Keeler just now. More than anything, I thought, he wanted us gone and forgotten.

Cherry Benjamin arrived. Her gum boots were dirty and the shapeless clothes made her look old. She looked different from the witness Jake, with misplaced confidence, had called earlier.

"I'd like her sworn again," I said. "Just to make certain she understands the oath."

Keeler raised his eyebrows. Normally an admonition to the witness that she was still under oath would have sufficed.

"Raise your right hand," the judge ordered docilely. "Do you solemnly swear that the testimony you give will be the truth, the whole truth, and nothing but the truth, so help you God?"

Cherry looked at me and at Keeler. "I do." She smiled oddly at me and said conversationally, "I thought you were dead. I prayed for you. There were stories around."

"You're the same Cherry Benjamin who testified previously in this case?" I asked, ignoring her remarks.

"Yes."

"And, at that time, you were asked whether or not your ex-husband, Avery Benjamin, was dead or alive."

"I was."

"And you stated you knew he was dead."

"I did, and I also know he died in a fire at his home that was once my home."

"Tell the jury how long ago your ex-husband died, Mrs. Benjamin."

"A long time ago."

"How long?"

"I'm not very good with time. Each day is a century if you do wrong things, a moment if you stay with the Good Book."

"And Avery Benjamin died in a fire?"

"Yes, he did. That's a fact."

"At the home he occupied also with your successor, Hilda Benjamin?"

She turned away from me and smiled at Hilda. "Yes, he did." Her smile was almost friendly.

I was undaunted and not particularly puzzled. "And you're telling me the exact truth now?"

"Of course I am." Her eyes watched me and suddenly a new realization came to me. I had a little further insight. I remembered something I'd recently seen and imagined a little bit more about what had happened.

"Were there two fires there at that house or only one, Mrs. Benjamin?"

"In the house? One fire is all I know about."

"On the property including the garage?"

She thought about it. She looked at me trying to see what I

knew. "I don't know how many fires there were. Two maybe. More."

I moved on for the moment. "Who told you I was dead, Mrs. Benjamin?"

She shrugged. "Any number of people. This is a small town, Mr. Robak. Rumors pass around quickly here."

"When I came to town last Friday, did you watch me arrive, Mrs. Benjamin?"

She hesitated and then nodded. "Yes. I did that. Your partners told me they'd called you, so I came and watched you for a while. I was interested in you and—curious. I read a story about you once in a newspaper."

"And did you tell your sons I'd arrived?"

"I mentioned you. I had breakfast with them soon after you'd arrived and I told them."

"Were they the first to tell you I'd died?"

"Not died, exactly. Disappeared may have been the word they used."

Damon Lennon was on his feet. "I fail to see what Mr. Robak's situation, no matter how interesting it is to him, has to do with the instant case, your honor."

Judge Keeler watched me out of faraway eyes. The courtroom smelled of wet sweat and too many people in a closed space with a defective heating plant.

"I trust you plan to tie this into something, Mr. Robak?"

"Yes, your honor. If the court will allow me a bit more leeway, things may become clear."

"And this has to do with the case in question—did Avery Benjamin die in the house fire at his home?" he asked. He wiped his forehead. The courtroom was warm.

"Yes." I smiled at Cherry Benjamin. "And also the time frame and the circumstances concerning how he died."

"All right. Proceed."

Damon Lennon sat down and shook his head, puzzled both with me and the court.

"Did your sons tell you how I'd died or disappeared, Mrs. Benjamin?"

"Only that you'd not be around anymore."

"And you believed them?"

She wiggled a little in her chair. "Oh yes. I always believe them. They're my sons."

"Did they tell you they tried to burn me to death night before last in one of their storage buildings?" I asked softly.

Lennon was up. "Now this is about it, your honor. Mr. Robak knows better than this. We're going to move for a mistrial now, much as it pains us so to do. And some sanctions against Mr. Robak and his partners."

I saw Jake moving restlessly in his chair and I nodded at him confidently. Steinmetz whispered to him and then gave me a short nod.

Judge Keeler nodded also. He watched me cautiously.

"We'll join in the motion for a mistrial in a bit," I conceded. "For now I'd like to continue with this witness. Maybe some questions will get solved as to the necessity for sanctions or another trial."

Keeler looked out at the newsmen sitting attentively in the courtroom and down at me.

"Continue," he said heavily.

I turned back to Cherry Benjamin. "You belong to a church and believe in its teachings, don't you, Mrs. Benjamin?"

"I do," she said stoutly. "Belonging to the Most Holy Redeemer Church has changed my life and cleansed it. I'm no longer a heavy user of spirits. When I do fall from grace, the Lord helps me to quickly recover."

"Do you still use alcoholic beverages?"

"A bit of wine for inspiration—to see things more clearly. That's not forbidden."

"At one time, were you a drinking companion to Ray Lucas, who once represented the defendants in this case?"

"Yes. I knew Ray. He was killed."

"How did he die?"

"In a car."

I abandoned that for the moment. "So now you believe and are born again in the Lord?" I asked, watching.

"I am." Her face became radiant with a beatific smile.

"And so you must tell the truth. You did so the other day when you were on the stand, didn't you?"

"I most certainly did."

"But you left some things out?"

She shrugged. "I told the truth. I gave strict answers to the questions I was asked."

"All right. Did you follow me through the woods across from the nuclear plant and fire a gun at me?"

"I did. You'd invaded my property, my home in the woods."

"Your home or your ex-husband's home?"

"His once, but mine now."

"How long since he stayed there?"

"Time is relative," she said.

"But you admit you followed me in your four-wheel-drive Jeep and then fired a gun at me? Twice?"

"Only to frighten you, Mr. Robak. You weren't hurt."

"And then, two nights ago, did you fire your gun through the window of the motel where I'm staying?"

"I did that," she said righteously. "You and those others had come to town to steal from my sons, and you were drinking and carousing with liquor around you. My ex-husband was dead and you were celebrating your misdeeds. So I fired my rifle to show you that both the Lord and I were watching." She shook her head gently. "Again, no one was hurt. And one day soon I'll pay that evil motel up there for their window."

"Your sons told me they'd set fire to many homes including one where a child died. Did you know that?"

"They never told me," she answered, voice full of pain. She

looked down and away and I saw there was something I wasn't getting in her answer.

"But you suspected it, didn't you?"

"Yes. I suspected they were setting fires. I knew the fires were set. Anyone would know. The whole county knew."

"Did your sons ever threaten you?"

She shook her head. "Not me."

Once again I knew there was more. "But they did tell you something that bothered you, didn't they? Was it about their father?" I watched her face. Nothing.

"No," I said, realizing what it was. "It was your church. Was that it? Did they threaten to do something to your church? To the church of the Most Holy Redeemer?"

She looked away and then back. "I knew they were bad when they did that, said that, so I prayed for them each night."

"And do you pray for Avery also?"

"Of course. Almost every night."

"For how long?"

Her eyes went vague again. "A long time now."

"One month?" I asked.

She nodded.

"How about two months?"

She looked away. "Time is relative," she said again.

"Wasn't Avery Benjamin alive until two months or so ago? Today is the first of November. Was he alive, for example, alive in August of this year?"

She looked at me and out around the courtroom. She saw someone back there and I followed her gaze. The man in the rear was large and old and dressed in funereal black. I'd never seen him before, but I made a bet with myself he was the preacher at the Most Holy Redeemer Church.

"He was alive," she whispered. "He was alive."

"Until you killed him? Didn't you kill him?"

She looked down at the floor. "He was evil. He made me

meet him in the woods and sleep with him after he had another woman. After we were divorced. And I was weak in things of the flesh."

"But he was alive and evil. Until about two months or perhaps a bit less ago."

She nodded. "Yes."

The courtroom had been very still as the spectators strained to hear what we were saying. Now, in the back, a man I vaguely recognized as a reporter got quickly up and headed for the door. Judge Keeler ignored him.

"And you knew you had to testify and that you had to tell the truth, so in Avery's killing you made it like it was originally. You took him to the old place, the old burned place where he'd lived with you and then with Hilda. And you set him afire in the garage." I watched her. "Isn't that the way it was?"

"Yes. I did that. That was the very night I talked with the Lord. Since then I've been his handmaiden, his servant." She smiled sweetly. "And my God believes in vengeance. Read the book. I believe He doesn't need lawyers or doctors and abhors the things of the flesh."

"And what happened to Avery's body?"

"I gave it a Christian burial. I read Scripture over it." Her eyes were bright and innocent. In her mind she was sane and right. In mine she was not.

"I see."

"I told Avery I had to see him about the insurance and about what Hilda was doing, and so we met where we'd lived once. I planned it that way. He wanted to meet in the woods, but that wasn't to be. Not again in his sleeping bag that I washed five times afterward to cleanse it. I hit him and threw gasoline on him and set him afire in the garage."

"Where did the first body come from—the one they thought was Avery?"

"Somewhere. Avery found him. Maybe he and Hilda went

away and found someone. Avery threatened me that if I told anyone, I'd die. But I wasn't afraid. Not of him. Maybe of the darkness coming. But so many go there." She smiled wisely. "All of us, Mr. Robak. You also."

I shuddered inwardly and looked up at the judge and he nodded at me. It wasn't a friendly nod, but it was enough. I glanced at Damon Lennon. There needed to be a bit more for him.

"You know your sons tied me up and tried to burn me in a fire they set night before last?"

"No. I didn't know that."

"They did do it."

"I believe you. Somehow I know you won't lie to me." She waggled a finger at me like a schoolteacher to a wayward youth. "Never do that, Mr. Robak. They were good boys," she said. A tear came at the corner of each eye. "But he let them grow up wrong. And he had his women and his dirty money and his cronies to split it up with."

"And you took some of it at the divorce."

She shook her head. "I took as little as I could when we were divorced. But then, when he was going to make my boys rich, he had to be the perpetual joker and go wandering around and Ray Lucas saw him. So Avery set a trap for Ray and ran his car off Cemetery Hill. No one else knew, but I did, because Avery told me, taunted me. He said that he was divorced, but I wasn't. He didn't like me seeing Ray." She shook her head. "He didn't like lawyers. So he killed Ray so that Hilda and the boys would get the money. He was clever. He took a piece of metal and rubbed it against that tree at the top of the hill to make it look like Ray's car had grazed it. No one suspected until you came along, Mr. Robak. And when Hilda turned Avery away, he came to me."

"How did Ray's death make you feel?"

"After Avery killed Ray, I knew I was going to punish him. But I knew that somehow, for my boys, that the way he died

had to be like the way he'd already pretended to die, or when
I was called to testify I'd give it all away. So I used a hammer
and then gasoline on him. Then I buried him near the hole by
the Blue where we used to go to hunt and fish—his place.
Now it's mine. And his—forever—"

I went back to a chair and sat down. It was half past nine in
the morning and I was already dog-tired. I looked at the old
lady on the stand and she beamed at me. She sat in her old
clothes and gum boots and was on top of the world. I knew
that the insanity she owned was one that was spreading.
She'd taken the law and God into account in her plans and
made them a part of her scheme.

They prosper. God (their version) is good. Law, which in-
terferes in their beliefs, is evil. They clog the system like
locusts. And they plan against all.

"I have no more questions." I looked over at Damon Lennon politely. He shook his head, a wounded fighter. I sat
down.

There were a few more things that happened. The next
week, on the cold morning after the fall election, I got a call
from Drewville. It was Ted Powers, the high school kid
who'd coordinated the woods search and the rest for me.

"Good to hear from you," I said.

"Thought you might want to know," he said. "About everyone who ran for reelection up here got beat bad. Two
commissioners, the treasurer. The big newspapers never did
let up on anyone around here, and there've been state audi-
tors and federal people all over since you left. Damon Lennon's called the grand jury and they're interested in the extra
body found in the Benjamin house two years ago."

"They should be. How about Judge Keeler? Did he win?"

"Lost. By about two hundred votes. And the jail's still full
of Benjamins. They say that Fritz, the crazy one, is babbling a
lot of names. They say he also thinks you're big magic of some

kind." He was silent for a long moment. "Some of us were talking. We'd like to know how you figured it, Pops."

"Hunches more than anything else."

"Just hunches?"

"Luck. A couple of good guesses. A few facts. Mainly a lady who murdered her ex-husband and then saw the light and joined a church where she felt she could tell no lies. I became sure Avery Benjamin hadn't died when Hilda's house went up a couple of years back. Avery was just a joker with an anger at the insurance industry because he thought he'd been cheated. So he tried to outsmart them and rub their noses in it at the same time. Thereafter it was just trying to find someone who'd tell me when he *did* die. So I put Cherry in a situation where she had to tell me. She thought she was safe when Jake got done. When I put her back on the witness stand it was confession time and she did just that."

"She's crazy," he said.

"Positively."

"But how did you know it was her?"

"I thought it might be the boys all the way through. I even thought it might be Hilda and the sheriff. But there was only a single sleeping bag in the hiding hole I found—that you found for me—and that ruled out the boys. Besides, they still thought that Avery Benjamin was alive."

"They know now," he said. "They dug him up the day after you left. No doubt this time."

"The hole was neatly kept—a woman's touch. There wasn't any booze there. That meant Cherry. And there were flammable liquids in old booze bottles, probably Ray Lucas's old scotch bottles."

"I heard she'd said that."

"But most of all it was the second fire at the burned-out house. Why would anyone do that unless that someone thought she might be asked, knew she had to tell the truth, and so made it again like what it was supposed to have been?

And no one had seen Avery for a while and Cherry changed her testimony on the witness stand." I thought some more. "How about Hilda and your fine sheriff?"

"He took a vacation. No one's seen her. Rumors around town are that that they left together. Rumors also say she took a suitcase full of money along. No one really knows. It's a small town."

"My, my," I said. I decided not to tell him about the holes I'd dug in her yard to bother her. They obviously had.

His voice was curious. "Do you ever feel sorry for Cherry and for what you did to her in the courtroom?"

"No. She'd made a bargain with herself about truth. I knew she'd tell it if I could ask the right questions. So I asked them. I pinned her down. There were a couple of things I didn't go into on the witness stand because there was no need. I'll let Damon Lennon think on them. Not me anymore. She said she didn't know about the boys, her sons, and the fires. She was being truthful to the question I asked. But she had to see those fire devices her sons kept in her hidey-hole. The place was too neat for her not to have noticed them." I thought for a moment. "She's a woman who uses the truth, not one who sees it. I was never positive Avery Benjamin was dead until she finally told her whole story on the witness stand. I didn't know what I was going to get out of her when I called her." I sighed. "That's about all of it."

"Thank you for talking to me," he said. He was silent for a long moment. "I may try pre-law next year at the university there in Bington. Can I come see you if I do?"

"Sure. Just don't call me Pops in the office or around my wife or son."

"You've got a son?" he asked as if surprised. "How old?"

"Three years old."

"Now that's truly a miracle for the wise men," he said. "So long, Pops."

About the Author

Joe L. Hensley has written for many magazines, in both the science fiction and mystery fields. He is the author of ten Crime Club selections, including *Final Doors*, a collection of short stories. Judge Hensley lives in Madison, Indiana.